Change

Treesong

Thank you for supporting change!

Treesong

Cranncheol Publishing

CHANGE

Copyright © 2013 Treesong.

All rights reserved.

Published by Cranncheol Publishing.

ISBN: 0615806066
ISBN-13: 978-0615806068

Cover design by Acaisha Buffo.

This book is dedicated
to everyone who has taken action
in response to anthropogenic global warming
and to the future generations
of human and non-human life
who will inherit the world
created by our choices.

ACKNOWLEDGMENTS

The road to Change has been long and winding. I could fill an entire book with thank yous for everyone who has helped me along the way.

Thank you to my mother and father for bringing me into this world, caring and providing for me to the best of your ability, and educating me with your words and deeds about how to be a good person and live a good life. I am deeply saddened that you are not here to celebrate the publication of this novel. However, I believe that you are with us in spirit. Your memory lives on in the hearts of many who knew you. We had some difficult times, but we also some wonderful times. Any good that I do in this life was surely made possible by your love and guidance.

I would also like to thank the rest of my family. Thank you to my stepfather, Don, for helping to support us and building a new family with us. Thank you to my brother, Errol, for always being there for me. I've rarely said so, but your thoughtfulness, kindness, dedication to your studies, concern for social justice, and basic human decency have always been an inspiration to me. Thank you to my sister, Valerie, for appreciating me, going on adventures into other worlds with me, and always sharing your writing and music and dreams with me, even when I hadn't yet learned to appreciate them. Watching you grow from a tiny infant into an amazing woman helped inspire me to do what I can to make the world a better place for future generations. Also, thank you to my extended family for many fun childhood memories, including visits to local forest preserves and Graue Mill with my grandfather. Walking in the woods encouraged my environmental awareness at an early age.

Thank you to the many members of the Student Environmental Center, Friends of Bell Smith Springs, R.A.C.E., Heartwood, the Cove Mallard Coalition, and others who introduced me to the Shawnee Forest, the Nez Perce Forest, and a variety of local, regional, national, and global environmental issues. Your education, mentoring, and friendship helped me to transform from a timid recluse into an environmental superhero.

Thank you to the many friends and colleagues who have inspired me. Thank you to Aur Beck for being a friend, introducing me to the radio show and community, and helping me to stay energized. Thank you to Sarah Kemp for being my friend and yoga teacher. Thank you to Courtney Hahn, Steve Hahn, Daniel St. Francis Xavier Hessian Raino, Rhiannon O'Neal, Christopher "Eel" Williams, Travis Baker, Brandon Guess, Ben Simpson, Ryan Favier, Jennifer Melfi, Joshua Guess, and others for adventuring with me and introducing me to new realms of fantasy and science fiction. Thank you to R. Michael Fisher for the fearology and integral praxis and Zach Seibert for the magic and poetry. Thank you to Sarah Mae Paull and her friends and family for the weekly dinners and game nights that helped me keep my sanity and feel welcome.

Thank you to Gaia House Interfaith Center and everyone who I've met there. This amazing community center is a crossroads where people of all faiths, beliefs, and backgrounds come together to break bread, share stories, explore their spirituality, and seek environmental and social justice. It was the first place I ever attended an environmental event and the main reasons I stayed in Southern Illinois. It has been my honor and pleasure to serve the Gaia House community in a variety of ways.

Thank you to the many authors of science fiction and fantasy who have inspired me with their creative vision and passion for developing fantastic worlds, characters, and stories. This includes pioneers such as Isaac Asimov, Aldous Huxley, George Orwell, Kurt Vonnegut, and Robert Heinlein, and more recent inspirations such as Starhawk, Neil Gaiman, Phil "Satyros" Brucato, and Richard Garriott.

Last, but certainly not least, I would like to thank my girlfriend, Grace, for being with me during the final stages of completing this novel. Your presence in my life has brought me the happiness, inspiration, and motivation I needed to finish a project that was several years in the making. I love you and am blessed to have you in my life.

KICKSTARTER ACKNOWLEDGMENTS

This novel was made possible in part by a Kickstarter campaign. Kickstarter is a crowdfunding website where people propose creative projects and ask for backers to pledge their support. If there are enough total pledges to meet the goal by the deadline, the project is funded.

Thank you to the following people for your support:

Aur 'daenergymon' Beck
Jessica Bradshaw
Andi Darnell
Retha Daugherty
Don Ellis
Kimberly Ellis
Wes Foskey
Joshua Guess
Stephen & Courtney Hahn
Melissa Hubbard
Heather Jacob
Tim Kirkpatrick
Leaf Lad
Joel R. Landry
Hugh
F & J Murphy
Julia Murphy
Errol O'Neill
Auntie Kristie
Ben, Amy, and Kieran
Dinah Seibert
Jessie Sims
Katie Thomas
Lex van Vucht
Joshua Vaughn
ChristopherWilliams
Marisa

There were several backers who didn't respond to the backer survey. To err on the side of privacy, if a backer didn't respond to the survey, they are not listed above. I apologize if I missed anyone who wanted to be on this list.

There were also some backers who chose to remain anonymous. Even though you are not recognized in this list, you still have my personal thanks and a share in the credit for making this possible.

Your pledge to this project not only supported this novel, but also supported the emergence of a world in which artists describe their creative vision to the public and everyone who likes that vision can participate in making it a reality.

CHAPTER 1

*"Death is in the air.
Chariot out of control.
Change is awakened."*
— Bertram Muhnugin, The Death of Birth

    Sarah opened her eyes and rose out of her crouching stance.
    It had all happened so fast. An aging silver Dodge Dynasty had come crashing through the railing of the overpass and into the crosswalk below. Sarah had reflexively thrown her arms in front of herself and ducked down, knowing full well that she couldn't stop the several ton hunk of metal hurtling in her direction.
    But somehow, she had.
    Sarah's heart was still racing as she scanned her surroundings. The formerly airborne sedan sat motionless in the street just a few feet in front of her. It was mostly intact, aside from a shattered windshield and some compression of the front end of the frame.
    The other half-dozen people in the crosswalk behind her slowly emerged from their own protective stances and stared at the car in wonder. An old man on the other side of the intersection was looking back and forth between Sarah and the car, his eyes and mouth wide in wonder. After a few moments, he started clapping slowly. Soon, everyone around the intersection joined him.

"How did you do that?"

Sarah looked down at her hands, dumbfounded.

"I don't know. I didn't even touch it. I—" She looked back at the car, wiping the sweat from her brow. "I guess I just willed it to stop." She shook her head in disbelief, turning back to the old man across the street. "I really stopped it?"

The old man nodded and started walking toward her slowly. "Lady, that old junker was about to rip your head off and land across the street. You stopped it in midair. Damnedest thing I ever seen."

"Really?" Sarah turned back to the wreckage, shaking her head again. "I wish I'd kept my eyes open."

The people around her burst into uneasy laughter. Sarah's heart was still racing, but she chuckled too.

"Is everyone all right?"

The bystanders looked around. Nobody seemed hurt. The car had landed in the street without hitting anyone. The driver stepped out of the car and examined it carefully, looking even more confused than the people in the crosswalk.

Sarah and a few of the other pedestrians walked around the car slowly, making sure that no one had been crushed beneath it. After a few minutes, several police cars and an ambulance arrived, followed by a news van.

An officer with a notepad stepped out of the nearest police car. He spoke first with the driver of the Dynasty, then with a few of the other pedestrians. Finally, he shook his head, took a deep breath, and walked over to Sarah.

"Ma'am, I'm Officer Harold of the Gorton Police Department. Mind if I ask you a few questions?"

Sarah laughed nervously. "Sure, why not?"

Officer Harold nodded. "Your name?"

"Sarah Athraigh. Sarah with an H, Athraigh with an A-T-H-R-A-I-G-H. You can call me Sarah."

"Alright, Sarah. Can I see some ID?"

Sarah pulled out her wallet and showed the officer her driver's license. He wrote down her name and address in his notebook before handing the license back to her.

"Got it." He paused, lowering the notepad and looking

Sarah in the eye. "Look, Sarah, I'm not going to lie here. I'm a little skeptical about what these other people are telling me. So I'd like you to tell me, in your own words, what happened here."

Sarah laughed. "I wish I knew, Officer. I was just crossing the street, when suddenly this car crashed through the railing on the overpass. I covered my head, closed my eyes, and figured I was about to get hit. But then it just stopped."

"Huh. Just stopped?"

"In mid-air. I had my eyes closed, but in my mind's eye, I just saw the car stopping in mid-air — and it did!" She looked at the damaged car, then back at Officer Harold with another nervous laugh. "Officer, that car was about to plow right through me. But somehow, something stopped it. I don't know if it was something I did, or divine intervention, or what. But whatever it was, it saved my life."

Officer Harold nodded slowly. "Well, that's what they said too." He looked at her, then over at the car, then back at her again. "And where were you standing when the accident happened?"

Sarah looked down at the ground. "Right around here, officer. I took a quick look around the car to make sure everyone was all right, but then I came back to this spot."

Office Harold shook his head with a sigh. "Alright, Sarah."

He handed her a business card. "Here's my card. If you think of anything else — anything at all — please give us a call."

"Okay. Thanks, Officer."

Officer Harold started walking away, then turned back to her. "Oh, I almost forgot. There's a reporter here. Do you want to talk to her, or should I tell her to back off?"

Sarah thought about it for a moment. "It's fine, Officer. I'll go ahead and talk to her."

Officer Harold shrugged. "Alright, then." He turned away, reading his notebook and shaking his head as he walked back to his patrol car.

The reporter was a young woman in her mid-twenties

with shoulder-length blond hair and a black suit coat and skirt. She talked to a few of the other witnesses before walking up to Sarah, followed by her cameraman.

"Hi there! I'm Jenny Goodman with Channel 3 news. Mind if I ask you a few questions?"

Sarah smiled. "Sure, go ahead."

Jenny turned to the cameraman, and he raised his camera and pointed it at Sarah. Sarah smiled, adjusting her long black ponytail and green T-shirt as Jenny turned on the microphone.

"Okay, can you start by telling us your name and where you're from?"

"Sarah Athraigh from Gorton, Illinois."

"Okay, Sarah." Jenny paused, looking down at her notes. "Sarah, people on the scene of this accident are saying that what they witnessed today was a miracle. Do you agree? Was this a miracle?"

Sarah smiled, shaking her head slightly in exasperation. "I really don't know, Jenny. It happened so fast, and I don't know how to explain it."

"Witnesses say the car stopped in mid-air, just short of hitting you. Is that what really happened?"

"I think so." She paused for a moment, thinking back to the accident. "I closed my eyes when it was about to hit me. When I opened my eyes, it had stopped short and dropped to the ground. It definitely stopped in mid-air."

"Did the car hit you?"

"No." She paused again, looking over at the crumpled front end of the car. "I just visualized it stopping, and it stopped."

"Wow. That's... wow." Jenny laughed. "Sorry, I've just never covered a story like this before. I wish we had video of the accident!"

Sarah shrugged. "It all happened so fast, I doubt anyone caught it on video."

"That's what everyone else said, too." She looked at her watch, then nodded at the cameraman. "Anyway, Sarah, I've got to go get this to my producer in time for the 6 o'clock news. Can I get your number in case we have any more questions?"

"Sure."

After the two women exchanged numbers, Jenny said a quick goodbye and rushed off to her news van with cameraman in tow. Sarah looked around the accident scene for a few more moments, then glanced down at her watch.

"Late again."

Sarah looked around to see if anyone else had any questions for her. A few people who had been staring at her turned away when she looked at them, but no one was making any motions to approach her. After another quick glance at her watch, she looked both ways and finished crossing the street. Once she reached the far side of the street, she looked back over her shoulder for a moment, examining the accident scene one last time. Then, she shook her head and kept walking.

CHAPTER 2

*"Center abandoned.
Poet of old knows the way.
Change is coming now."
— Bertram Muhnugin, The Death of Birth*

The Student Ecology Center was located in the heart of downtown Gorton. The other lots on Main Street were home to a collection of restaurants and storefronts housed in tightly-packed brick or concrete buildings. The Center, however, was nestled in the midst of a two-acre green space between Main Street and the train tracks. This land featured a pond with a bubbling fountain, a vegetable garden, several species of trees, a small Japanese garden, and a two-story geodesic dome at the south end of the property. The partial canopy left the land cooler than its surroundings, and the lush vegetation filled the air with the scent of green leaves, moist soil, and the first few blossoms of Spring.

Sarah walked down the sidewalk toward the Center, casually glancing at the garden as she walked. She was wearing black cargo pants, hiking boots, and a simple forest green T-shirt. Her long black hair was pulled back into a ponytail, and her green eyes were shining brightly at the sight of her destination. As she turned down the cobblestone path to the front door of the Center, she was surprised to discover someone waiting for her. He was a young man in his mid-twenties with disheveled orange hair, sky blue eyes, bold freckles, a light blue button-up shirt, and navy blue cargo pants. For a moment, his expression was calm and introspective as he leaned against the door and looked off into the distance. As Sarah approached, however, his eyes met hers, and a sudden look of panic spread over his face.

"Oh Gods." He stood up straight, his eyes darting up and down the street behind Sarah. "I was almost hoping you'd left already. We have to go."

Sarah slowed to a stop a few yards from the man, a quizzical smile spreading across her lips. "Excuse me?"

"There's no time to explain. We have to go before they come for you."

Sarah chuckled, shaking her head with a slow smirk. "Do I even know you? A lot of people pass through here, and some of them have pretty unique takes on—"

He took a step forward, raising a hand to silence her. "I can explain along the way. We just need to go. It's not safe here."

Sarah crossed her arms in front of her chest, her smile fading and her eyes narrowing into a stone-cold glare.

"Do you have a name, sir?"

The man sighed in exasperation. "Taliesin."

"Taliesin? My name is Sarah." Her stern expression was softened by a slight smile. "For someone named after a poet, you sure don't have a way with words."

"I do on a good day." Taliesin relaxed a bit, staring off into the distance. "Today isn't a good day."

"I tell you what, Taliesin. I'm about to start my office hours here at the Center. Why don't you come on in and tell me what's up? If you convince me I need to go somewhere, I might be able to find someone to cover for me."

Taliesin nodded, taking a deep breath. "Fair enough." He stepped away from the door, standing in the grass to make room for Sarah to pass. "After you, then."

Sarah gave him a wary look, then stepped up to the door. After unlocking it, she propped it open with a nearby stone and stepped inside.

The inside of the Center had just as much of an open and earthy feel as the outside. The first floor was forty feet in diameter and was lit by natural light streaming in through several six-sided windows, a set of double glass doors, and a six-sided sunroof. Most of the first floor looked like one large living room, with two couches, three small tables, several stacks of chairs, a desk, and an office and bathroom in the back. The second floor was shaped like a ring, with a large opening in the center that allowed people on the first floor to see the sunroof overhead and the shelves of books that lined the walls upstairs.

Taliesin walked into the center of the room and turned around in a slow circle, examining every detail while Sarah walked over to the desk and sat down. After a few moments, Taliesin's attention snapped back to Sarah, and he strode briskly across the room to her desk.

"Have a seat."

Sarah indicated a chair to the left of the desk. Taliesin shook his head, dismissing her offer with a wave of his hand.

"No thanks."

"Fine, have it your way."

Taliesin paused, taking a long, slow breath.

"Sarah, I believe your life is in danger, or at least your freedom."

Sarah chuckled, her lips spreading into a broad grin.

"Is this about my student loans? I knew those would come back to haunt me eventually. Or is it another crackdown on environmentalists? I was worried the FBI had forgotten about me."

Taliesin's face flushed with frustration.

"Sarah, this is serious."

"Oh, don't mind me. I have a dark sense of humor." She paused, noticing the anxious expression on Taliesin's face. "Seriously though, why do you think I'm in danger?"

"I saw you on the news last night."

Sarah sat back in her chair and stared off into the distance, her face settling into a serious expression. Her thoughts flashed back to last night, replaying every moment of the accident and the interviews in her mind. When she'd woken up in the morning, it had all seemed like a dream. But the look of concern on Taliesin's face made it all seem very real.

"Last night was... strange." She paused, shaking her head with a sigh. "I still don't understand what happened. But what does it matter? I'm sure everyone just thinks I'm crazy. It's not like the Men In Black are going to come get me."

Taliesin laughed nervously. "Men In Black are an urban legend." His eyes darted around the room to make sure that they were alone. "But there are real people out there who don't like people like us."

"People like us?" She shifted in her seat uncomfortably. "Look, I don't know who you think you are, or who you think I am, but —"

Taliesin's eyes lit up with a flash of inspiration. He raised a hand to interrupt her.

"Do I have permission to heal you?"

Sarah stared at him blankly. A puzzled expression slowly spread across her face.

"Heal me?"

"Showing is quicker than telling. Do I have permission to heal you? I don't need to touch you, I can do it from where I'm standing."

"Hmm." Sarah thought for a moment, studying Taliesin's features carefully. "Sure."

Taliesin nodded.

"Stand up, please."

Sarah rose to her feet, a skeptical smile slowly spreading across her lips. Taliesin unbuttoned the top button of his shirt and pulled out a silver pendant on a leather necklace, clasping the pendant in his left hand and holding it over his heart. He raised his right hand, extending his palm toward Sarah. Then, he closed his eyes, and his whole body relaxed, a light smile spreading across his lips.

After a moment's pause, he started to sing.

*"The living soil heals me
The flowing water heals me
The blowing wind heals me
The dancing fire heals me."*

Taliesin's baritone voice was soft but powerful, effortlessly filling the room with its sweet melody. As he sang, Sarah felt a rush of warmth. It started in her heart, but quickly spread throughout her body.

*"Heal my body, heal my spirit
Mend my wounds and set me free.
Heal my body, heal my spirit
As I will it, so mote it be."*

Sarah felt a pleasant but almost feverish tingling sensation in her lower back, neck, hips, and left knee. Her eyes closed, and she relaxed fully into the unexpected wave of inner heat. Her breathing deepened, her posture improved, and tension she didn't even realize she was carrying melted away from her muscles and bones.

As the moment passed and the feeling faded, she realized that Taliesin had repeated his song several more times before falling silent. She opened her eyes, looking up to him with a sly smile.

"How did you do that?"

Taliesin grinned, tucking the pendant back into his shirt.

"Now do I have your attention?"

"Yes."

Taliesin paused a moment to compose his thoughts.

"Some of us have special abilities. In fact, we all do. But only some of us have learned how to activate these abilities."

Sarah crossed her arms, nodding thoughtfully as Taliesin continued.

"Different people have different ideas about what these abilities are and where they come from. Some of us try to study and develop them. Others try to…"

Taliesin trailed off in mid-sentence, his body tensing.

Sarah looked over his shoulder and noticed an unfamiliar figure walking in the door. It was a man in his mid-twenties with shoulder-length brown hair, a lime green shirt, khaki shorts, and sandals.

Sarah rose to her feet and stepped out from behind the desk.

"Hi!" Her smile was warm and genuine as she stepped forward. "How can I help you?"

"I was wondering if you have any books on organic gardening. I'm starting a new garden, and I saw the sign outside, so I thought you might be able to help me."

Sarah smiled. "You've come to the right place!" She pointed to the stairs. "There's a whole bookcase at the top of the stairs full of books about organic gardening. And I've got a garden myself, so let me know if you have any questions."

"Thank you." The man nodded politely and headed up to the library.

After waiting a few moments, Sarah turned back to Taliesin. She stepped closer to him and lowered her voice to a near whisper.

"So what you're saying is that someone's going to see my story on TV and come after me?"

"Yes. Definitely. It's just a matter of when."

Sarah smirked. "I'll bet I'm already on a few lists for my environmental work. I'm sure the government could care less about my detours into the Twilight Zone."

"Sarah, what happened to you is like nothing I've ever seen before. I've read stories about people like you, and I've even seen photos of people levitating cars, videos of people bending steel with their mind, that sort of thing. But I always thought those were hoaxes!"

His voice was starting to rise in excitement, but he lowered it again to a whisper.

"Sarah, people have disappeared for less than this. I'm part of an online network that follows these stories, stories about anomalous abilities and the extremes of human potential. We've seen over a hundred people disappear over the last two years."

Sarah crossed her arms again, shaking her head with

a smile.

"Even if you're right, what do you suggest I do? Run?"

"Yes. I know someone up in St. Louis who..."

Taliesin's voice trailed off. He looked upstairs, and Sarah followed his eyes to notice the man in the green shirt looking at them. As soon as they looked his way, he smiled politely and looked back down at the open book in his hands.

For a moment, Sarah and Taliesin looked at each other in wide-eyed silence. Taliesin nodded his head slightly in the direction of the door, and Sarah nodded slightly in approval. Then, Sarah spoke.

"Well, I'm stuck here for the next few hours, but I'll be happy to meet you after my shift. There's a coffeehouse downtown called Rumi's Dance. Have you heard of it?"

Taliesin nodded, a slight smile spreading across his lips. "Yes, I love their coffee. And their chocolate ginger cookies."

She nodded. "Alright, does 1:30 work for you?"

"Definitely." He paused a moment. "Don't even stop home first, though. Meet me there right away."

"Agreed. Well, it's been a pleasure meeting you." She shook Taliesin's hand and pulled out her phone. "Let me get your phone number and walk you to your car."

"Nice meeting you too, Sarah."

Sarah and Taliesin walked out the door, entering their numbers into each other's cell phones. When they reached the parking lot, Sarah followed Taliesin to his car and walked over to the passenger side.

"I'll text someone about locking up the building. Let's go."

As she got into the car, Sarah noticed the man in the green shirt stepping out of the building and casually glancing in their direction. When he saw the car starting to pull away, he glared and pulled out a cell phone, walking briskly toward the parking lot.

Sarah smirked. "That guy doesn't look too happy."

"No, he doesn't." Taliesin's already pale complexion was ashen, and his grip on the steering wheel was tight. "Now do you believe me?"

"Yes." Her expression turned somber, and she sank back into her seat, staring out the window. "So what now? I've got activist friends who've got my back, but I don't think they're ready for anything like this. I don't even know what this is."

"Don't worry, I've got a plan. Are you up for a trip to the woods?"

"The woods?" Sarah grinned. "Always. When I text my friend, though, I'm going to tell her our destination and your license plate number. No offense."

"Oh." Taliesin's face flushed slightly. "Yes, that's fine. That makes sense. I've got to make a few phone calls, but there's a place a few miles from here where we can get some supplies and..." He paused, searching for words. "Well, some help."

"Sounds good."

Sarah pulled out her phone and started texting. Taliesin pulled out his phone and started making calls. As they drove toward the edge of town, the old downtown storefronts gave way to the box store sprawl at the edge of town. After a few minutes of driving, the buildings started to become more sparse, and they found themselves cruising down a four-lane highway surrounded by trees.

CHAPTER 3

*"Daughter of Caitlyn
rekindling forgotten flames.
Change is in her hands."*
— Bertram Muhnugin, The Death of Birth

"So. Where are we headed?"

Taliesin and Sarah had been driving in silence for several minutes. A turn off of the highway had led them onto a quiet two-lane state route lined with rolling wooded hills, open farmland, and the occasional gas station, rusty metal barn, or aging farmhouse. Taliesin glanced over at Sarah, then looked back at the road.

"What are your thoughts on magic?"

"You mean real magic? I've got friends who are into that." She smiled. "Normally, I'd tease you about it, but given how this day's going, I think I'll listen."

Taliesin nodded. "There are many definitions for magic. Personally, I like this one: magic is the art and science of creating change in accordance with will."

"By that definition, just about any human technology would qualify as magic."

"Exactly." Taliesin grinned. "Most people in modern societies focus on using and developing material technologies. But—"

"I'm not so sure about that."

Taliesin raised an eyebrow.

"Really?"

"Yes, really. Sure, we've got a lot of fancy gadgets like cell phones and airplanes. But the main thing holding it all together is social engineering. Advertisers tell us what to buy and when to buy it. That's where they get the money to make all that plastic and electronic crap. Politicians and CEO's are the new wizards, if you ask me." She looked out the window. "And they use their magic to rule the world."

"Hmm." Taliesin nodded. "You make a good point. Keep in mind, though, that they use advanced electronic technology to deliver their message. Some of us, however, focus on purely psychological and spiritual technologies." He touched his silver pendant through the fabric of his shirt. "You can call it psychic abilities, or magic, whichever you prefer. I call it both."

The car turned onto a gravel road that led into a denser stretch of woods. It was a sunny day, but as the tree branches met overhead, the clear blue sky was obscured by a patchwork of green leaves. Beams of sunlight filtered through the leafy canopy, and as the wind picked up, a swirling pattern of sun and shadow danced across the winding gravel road that stretched before them.

"My friend Morgan has land out here. She's High Priestess of my Coven, the Coven of the Living Soil." He shook his head with a soft smile. "We always joked about meeting up here in the event of an apocalypse. Now's our chance, eh?"

They turned onto a narrow dirt road that led up a fairly steep hill. After a few twists and turns, the road ended in a small grassy field. The far side of the field was filled with several cars and a big red pickup truck with two muddy ATVs in the back.

"This is the place."

Taliesin pulled in next to the truck and switched off the engine. He put on the parking break and opened the door, pausing a moment to stretch. As Sarah got out of the car, a lone figure stepped out of the woods and started heading their way.

"Tally Ho!"

The newcomer was a tall, heavyset, middle-aged man with short black hair, dark blue eyes, an olive T-shirt, weathered blue jeans, and a broad grin.

Taliesin's eyes perked up when he saw the man, and his lips spread into a warm smile.

"Henry!"

Taliesin opened his arms wide and walked over to Henry. The two men embraced, with Henry giving Taliesin a few pats on the back.

"How's it going, Tal?" He stepped back from the embrace and looked over Taliesin's shoulder. "And who's the lovely lady?"

Sarah smiled, shaking her head slightly.

"I'm Sarah."

She reached out to shake his hand. Henry clasped her hand in his beefy, calloused palm, shaking it firmly.

"Pleased to meet you, Sarah. Name's Henry." He studied her carefully for a moment, then looked over to Taliesin. "Is she's the one the fuss is all about?"

Taliesin nodded. "Where's Lady Morgan?"

"Oh, she's already up at the Circle." The smile faded from Henry's face. "I've never seen her like this, Tal. She's been touched by Goddess only know what, and it won't let go of her." He shook his head, looking down at his feet with a sigh. "I don't know what you told her, but she can barely even speak."

Taliesin nodded and turned to Sarah. "Alright, let's go."

He started following Henry toward the edge of the field. Sarah followed a few steps behind, examining her surroundings as they walked into the woods.

The trees that lined the simple dirt path were typical of the upland forest mix found in the hills of Southern Illinois. A dense canopy of blackjack, post, and several other oak varieties dominated the broadly sloping hillside, along with the occasional hickory and a sparse understory. The air was thick with the scents of the woods, and Sarah heard several songbirds singing along with the leaves rustling in the wind.

After a few minutes of walking, they emerged into another clearing. The opening in the canopy was about the size of a football field, but roughly circular, covered in a mix of grass and clover and the occasional patch of daisies or wildflowers. The left half of the clearing was home to a small wooden cabin with big windows, wooden shingles, and a simple sheet metal shed a few yards from the back door. The right half was home to a dirt circle with four simple wooden tables at the cardinal directions and four large stones at the cross-quarters. A large wooden altar stood at the center of the circle, and several people were gathered around the altar.

Henry, Taliesin, and Sarah approached the altar in silence. The four women and two men standing in the circle were dressed in a casual mix of jeans and T-shirts, but their expressions were anything but casual. Their eyes were closed, their hands were joined, and their voices were raised in song — a slow, mournful dirge that sent a chill down Sarah's spine.

> *"Blood of the womb bereft of child*
> *Death of rebirth and death of the wild*
> *Mother of life whose life was taken*
> *Be with us now, for we are forsaken."*

The people in the circle repeated the chant over and over again, their voices thundering deep and loud across the clearing and throughout the surrounding woods. Taliesin instinctively reached out for Sarah's hand, squeezing it lightly. He leaned over to whisper in Sarah's ear.

"They're not usually like this. They usually sing such happy and—"

"ATHRAIGH!"

Everyone fell silent in response to the sudden shout of the High Priestess. Taliesin jumped in place slightly and clenched Sarah's hand tightly. Sarah felt her heart race in her chest as the High Priestess stared at her in wonder, raising a finger to point in her direction.

"Sarah Athraigh!"

The High Priestess was a woman in her late thirties with deep brown eyes and long, wavy brown hair that moved lightly in the wind. She pointed at Sarah with a wild look in her eyes, stepping forward to place her free hand on the altar.

"Daughter of Caitlyn, Keeper of the Sacred Flame! If you would hear my words, step forward and enter this Circle!"

Sarah looked at Taliesin. A look of panic spread across Taliesin's face. He looked back and forth between Sarah and the High Priestess with an anxious shrug. Henry stared at Sarah with wide eyes for a moment before beckoning her toward the Circle with a nod of his head. After a moment's pause, Sarah took a deep breath, looked straight at the High Priestess, and stepped toward the Circle.

As Sarah entered the Circle, everyone but the High Priestess walked back to the stones around the edge of the Circle. Sarah stepped forward and stood across the altar from the High Priestess, bowing slightly before looking up at her expectantly.

The High Priestess stared at Sarah intently, studying her from head to toe and looking deeply into her eyes for the span of several heartbeats. Then, she closed her eyes and rested her hands lightly on the altar.

A sudden change came over the High Priestess. She rose to a full, proud stance, adopting a confident posture that seemed at once impossibly elegant yet completely relaxed and effortless. Her face softened into a light smile, and she stared directly into Sarah's eyes even though her own eyes were closed.

"You may not recognize me, child of Caitlyn, but I recognize you. Your mother prayed that I might watch over you in her stead. I have always been with you, though you knew not my name."

The wind picked up suddenly, sweeping a deck of Tarot cards off of the altar and scattering them through the air. A single red candle was lit on the altar, its flame unmoved by the wind. Sarah stared down at the candle for a moment, transfixed by the steady rhythmic swaying of the flame. She looked up at the High Priestess as if to ask a question, but then the High Priestess continued.

"The Change is upon us, my child. The flame that once lit your people's way through the cold and dark of winter now sears through the flesh of life itself. Your alchemists have set the world ablaze, harnessing the fury of countless explosions to drive steel chariots across land and sea and sky. Blades tempered by this insatiable fire hack whole families of creatures into oblivion. The smoke of this fire chokes the air with noxious fumes and fills the lands and waters of the world with a ferocious and feverish churning."

Suddenly, the red candle exploded and the surface of the altar burst into flames. Sarah's eyes opened wide as she reflexively took a step back, staring down at the flaming altar. When she looked back up at the High Priestess, the woman seemed undisturbed by the heat of the fire, and her closed eyes met Sarah's gaze.

"So many souls have been driven from this world too quickly. The cacophony of their keening is shredding the Veil. Your towers of fire and lightning and steel are a legion of blades stabbing through the tattered fabric of a dying world. Powers and principalities play games of strategy and sport amidst the seething carnage. They vie for the throne of a kingdom built on the fleshless bones of the death of rebirth."

By this point, the entire altar was consumed by a raging, crackling fire. Even though she was arm's length away, Sarah felt the heat of the fire on her skin. She also noticed that the High Priestess' clothes had started to singe and burn, though her hands and body seemed unharmed by the flames.

"Listen well, Sarah! If you would save this world, you must travel to the far corners of this land at the heart of the Change. You must journey with the priest who brought you to this Circle. You must find the woman who sings and dances with machines, the self-made hero beneath the tall tower, the sacred bard of blue and green, and the woman of state whose lover was lost to the Change. Together, you must find the mad prophet, face the mad king, and kindle the only flame that burns stronger and brighter than the mad conflagration that consumes this world."

Suddenly, the High Priestess collapsed, crumbling into a heap at the foot of the altar. For a moment, everyone stared at her prone form in silence. Then, one of the other women standing in the Circle leapt forward and started pulling the High Priestess away from the altar to protect her from the flames. Sarah looked on in stunned silence as the others in the Circle followed suit, reaching out to lift the woman's limp body and carry her toward the cabin. She was still breathing but seemed to be unconscious. As her people carried her out of the Circle, one of them cast a wary glance in Sarah's direction before looking back over at the cabin.

Harry and Taliesin whispered to each other for a moment. Harry headed back to the house and Taliesin started walking toward the Circle. Sarah snapped back out of her trance for long enough to wave Taliesin off in the direction of the cabin. Then she returned her attention to the center of the Circle, staring in silence at the crackling, flickering flames as they consumed the weathered wood of the altar.

CHAPTER 4

*"Heavier than stone,
the words can not be lifted.
Change must find a way."*
— Bertram Muhnugin, The Death of Birth

"Lemonade?"

Sarah was sitting on one of the large stones at the edge of the Circle, staring in silence at the stone opposite her. The altar had long since burned down into a pile of smoldering ashes and charred wood. When she heard Taliesin's voice, she looked up and accepted the glass he was handing her.

"Thanks."

She drank a few sips of the lemonade, glancing up at Taliesin with a light smile before returning her gaze to the stone.

"You alright?"

Sarah laughed, shaking her head.

"Believe it or not, I was trying to move that stone with my mind."

Taliesin chuckled.

"How's that working out for you?"

"Not well. Maybe it'll work better if you throw it at me."

Taliesin smiled.

"Good idea. But I wouldn't want to risk it."

He sat down on the ground next to Sarah. For several long minutes, the two sat together in silence, looking off into the distance. The wind was bringing in more clouds, turning the sky overcast and enveloping the sun. Sarah finished the lemonade, then set the glass down on the ground at her feet and spoke.

"I had just wrapped my mind around the idea of telekinesis." She turned to Taliesin with a glimmer in her eye, holding her index finger and thumb an inch apart from each other. "I was this close to accepting the fact that I had stopped a car with the power of my mind. And now this." She rose to her face, turning to face Taliesin. "Some sort of goddess was speaking through that woman, right? A goddess, the goddess? I don't even know what to call her."

Taliesin stood up and smiled, placing a hand on Sarah's shoulder.

"It's okay, Sarah. I've been doing this all my life, and I've never seen anything like that either."

She laughed, brushing away his hand with her own.

"How does that make it okay? Are we going crazy? Or did the shit just hit the fan?"

Taliesin reached out to Sarah again, more slowly and carefully this time, placing his fingertips lightly on her elbow.

"That was a Goddess named Bríd, or Brighid. Our High Priestess does a lot of work with her — channeling, divination, et cetera." He glanced down at the smoldering altar, then looked back at Sarah. "I've never seen anything like that, of course. But it was definitely Bríd."

Taliesin unbuttoned the top button of his shirt, pulling out his leather necklace with its silver pendant. The pendant was a triquetra, a series of three interwoven arcs joined at the ends to form a three-pointed symbol. He looked down at it for a long moment, then clenched it in his hand as he continued.

"This changes everything. I was just going to drop you off with a friend in St. Louis, but now I'm going with you."

"Really?" Sarah looked at the charred altar, then

looked back at Taliesin. "I don't mean to sound ungrateful here. Something bizarre and amazing just happened, and it's a relief to know you'll be coming with me. But—" She paused, struggling for words. "But like you said, this changes everything. If there are gods and goddesses, then who or what are they? Are we supposed to be subservient to them? I can handle telekinesis, but I don't think I can handle being bossed around by my invisible friends."

Taliesin smiled, shaking his head with a chuckle. "Most of us call it psychokinesis, not telekinesis. And Bríd's not like that. Notice she didn't tell you what to do. She just shared information."

"Really? I seem to remember her saying 'must' a lot."

"If/then statement. If you want X, then you must do Y. It's your choice what to do with that information."

"Alright, alright. Good point." Sarah took a step back and walked a few paces, slowly circling around to the far side of the scorched altar. "It sounded to me like she was talking about climate change, so I can see why she picked me. I've been working on climate change for years now. But I've got a hard enough time convincing people about the urgency of the issue. Telling them a goddess sent me won't add to my credibility."

Taliesin chuckled. "Maybe not."

Sarah made her best effort to impersonate an exaggerated Chicago accent from the movie Blues Brothers. "We're on a mission from God."

Taliesin laughed. "Or a mission from Goddess."

Sarah smirked. "Goddess or not, I'm already committed to doing everything I can about climate change."

Taliesin smiled. "Bríd chose wisely, then."

"Even if I didn't care about the other species on the planet — which I do, by the way — there's still the fact that extreme weather events and rising oceans really don't bode well for the survival of our own species."

"Hmm." He looked down at the altar, then looked over at Sarah. "It's that bad? I've heard about climate change, but I didn't know how bad it was getting. Bríd made it sound like the end of the world."

"Life will go on." Sarah stared down at the charred wood at the center of the circle. "Life always finds a way. But life as we know it, that's a whole nother story." She chuckled, but her eyes were cold and her expression was grim. "The CO2 in the atmosphere is over 400 parts per million and rising. We need to get it back below 350. Otherwise, the Arctic will keep thawing, and the oceans will flood the coasts, and extreme weather events will shut down whole cities, creating millions of climate refugees and destabilizing the entire world."

Sarah walked back around the circle and stood right in front of Taliesin, looking him squarely in the eyes.

"And that's what the most optimistic models tell us."

Taliesin chuckled anxiously.

"Well, we'd better get to work then." Taliesin glanced down at his watch. "We've still got time to make it St. Louis tonight, maybe even before dark. Do you want to leave now?"

Sarah glanced over at the cabin.

"Is your High Priestess alright?"

Taliesin smiled and nodded. "Oh, she's fine. She's awake and alert again. She's still feeling weak though, so she's lying down on the couch. She said to say hi."

"Glad she's okay." Sarah smiled for a moment, then her expression grew somber. "That was a little scary."

"A little?" Taliesin laughed. "Don't get me wrong, I love Bríd, she's my Goddess, she's amazing. But I was shaking!" His eyes grew wide, and he grabbed Sarah's hands. "Did you see her hands? She held her hands in the fire and they didn't burn! I've healed someone's burns before, but that takes a while. She held her hands in that fire like it was nothing!"

"Yeah, I kinda noticed. I had a front row seat."

"I know! And you just took it in stride!" He laughed. "That was pretty amazing. Oh, and it sounds like your mother was a follower of Bríd. Is that true?"

"I..." Sarah paused. "My mother was named Caitlyn. She died when I was a little kid. I don't remember her very well, but she was a devout Catholic."

"Ah." Taliesin let go of her hands, looking down at the scorched altar, lost in thought. "Well, the Catholics have a saint named after Bríd. I've heard she's really big in Ireland. There's even a group of nuns who have rekindled Saint Brigid's sacred flame."

"Interesting."

The two stared silently at the pile of ashes and scorched wood at the center of the circle for several long moments. Eventually, Sarah looked up at Taliesin with a broad smile.

"So. St. Louis then?"

Taliesin smiled. "Yes! I'll go say my goodbyes, and then we can go."

"Should I say goodbye too?"

"Hmm." Taliesin glanced over at the cabin, then back at Sarah. "It's alright, I'll go ahead and say goodbye for you."

Sarah smiled. "They're a little freaked out, aren't they?"

"Um, yeah. A little bit."

Sarah laughed. "Hey now, I'm not the one channeling goddesses and setting altars on fire."

Taliesin smiled. "Oh, it's nothing personal. And I'm sure they'll want to get to know you better later. They just need to spend a lot of time talking this out. And we need to spend that time on the road. Goddess only knows who's out there looking for you right now. We need to go."

"Alright then. Say goodbye for me. I'll meet you at the car."

"Sure thing."

Taliesin reached forward and gave Sarah a quick hug. Sarah hugged back, noticing a light minty scent on Taliesin before he let go and headed off toward the cabin at a brisk walk.

Sarah glanced up at the overcast sky, then stepped out of the circle for the first time since the High Priestess' prophecy. She turned back for a moment, extending her right hand into air as if to feel the invisible boundary. Her hand tingled slightly, and she thought she felt a hint of warmth and resistance as she reached across the unseen line at the edge of the stones. After a few moments of experimenting, she shook her head with a smile and started walking back to the car.

CHAPTER 5

*"Change is electric.
Science, art, ecstatic dance.
Technician of change."*
— Bertram Muhnugin, The Death of Birth

  The rush hour traffic on the aging bridge across the Mississippi River was slow and heavy as Taliesin and Sarah rode into St. Louis. A seemingly endless sea of cars, SUVs, pickup trucks, and semis moved slowly along the criss-crossing overpasses and underpasses like congested streams of metallic blood cells flowing through curving concrete arteries and veins. Billboards lined the edges of the highway, some of them changing their digital ads as the traffic ebbed and flowed. A few of the more run-down concrete and brick buildings near the bases of the supporting pillars were peppered with graffiti, while others had tidy painted exteriors or glimmering steel and glass facades towering high above the city streets below. The Gateway Arch was visible on the horizon for several long moments, then slipped behind the buildings as the overpass curved and Taliesin and Sarah continued their journey through the city.
  Sarah stared out the window in silence, watching the cars and cityscape go by. She had grown up in Southern Illinois, but only made it up to St. Louis once or twice a year, whenever there was a big protest or concert.

"So. Who's this person you know in St. Louis?"

"Her name's Patricia. Allegedly, she's part of an underground network called Anomalous Revolution. They—"

"Allegedly? You mean you haven't met her yet?"

"Well, not in person. We've talked a lot online, though. And there was that one time on the phone, but that was weird. Anyway, she was hard to track down because anyone who talks about Anomalous Revolution on the forums gets banned. Apparently, they're on some sort of Homeland Security watchlist."

"I know how that goes." Sarah shook her head with a sigh. "A few of my friends in Minneapolis had their house raided last year. Some people are really jumpy about environmental activists."

Taliesin nodded. "Have you ever been arrested?"

"Oh, yeah. Four times now." Sarah smirked. "But I earned at least three of those. That's what happens when you lock down at the headquarters of an oil industry thinktank, or do a treesit where someone's trying to build a road."

Sarah's expression grew more somber, her eyes filled with cold anger.

"I hate going to jail. I can't stand it. But if that's what it takes to slow them down, you do it, because somebody has to."

Taliesin nodded. "Looks like you made it back out."

"Yes!" Sarah laughed. "So far, anyway. I've been really lucky, actually. Maybe someone really is watching out for me."

Sarah looked out the window, a forlorn expression settling over her face. They rode together in silence for a few moments before she continued.

"They black bag people like us in the middle of the night, don't they? I've seen what the U.S. Government does to its own citizens. They send FBI spies into peace groups. I can't even imagine what they do to people who can move cars with their minds or make fire appear out of thin air."

"I can."

Sarah looked over at Taliesin, her eyes widening a bit in surprise. They exchanged a long, somber look. After a few moments, Taliesin returned his attention to the road, gripping the steering wheel tightly.

"Sorry. Anyway, yeah, not good. I don't want to end up at Guantanamo Bay, or some underground science lab. So let's hope Patricia can help us out here."

The two drove together for a while in silence. The off-ramp had taken them back down to ground level, and they found themselves driving through the streets of St. Louis beneath an overcast sky. After a few minutes of driving, they pulled up in front of Shameless Grounds, a three-story red brick building that looked abandoned aside from the coffee cup sign hanging above a windowless white door. After finding a parking spot near the coffee shop, they walked to the park that Taliesin's friend had designated as the meeting point.

The park was fairly small, with a baseball field, playground, and a few dozen trees that added a splash of vibrant green to a neighborhood that was otherwise filled with aging brick, creeping weeds, and broken blacktop. The playground equipment was colorful, modern, and inviting, but there was no sign of anyone else in the park at the moment. After circling the block without finding anyone, they decided to walk up the small flight of concrete steps leading to the playground,

As Sarah and Taliesin looked around, they both noticed a small brightly-colored object sitting on a park bench just past the playground. They gave each other a curious look, then continued forward slowly, studying the object carefully.

At first, it looked like an oversized garden gnome. As the two approached, however, it quickly became clear that this was no ordinary garden gnome. It was almost a foot tall, with a bright red hat that was just as tall as his body, a bright green shirt, bright red pants, and a long white beard. The clothing was made of actual cloth rather than ceramic or plastic, and the beard appeared to be made of cotton. The body was made of clear Plexiglas, with well-articulated hands and elaborate gears and circuitry visible beneath the transparent surface. The eyes were small lenses with retractable plastic shutters that served as eyelids. As Sarah and Taliesin approached, the gnome turned in their direction and looked up at them, cocking its head to the side slightly in curiosity.

"Hi there!"

The gnome's voice was oddly high-pitched and feminine given its long beard, but it was also surprisingly lifelike and melodic. Its Plexiglas jaw moved slightly as it spoke, crudely mimicking the words being spoken. As Sarah and Taliesin came to a stop a few feet away from the gnome, it turned to Sarah, looking her right in the eye.

"My name's David. What's your name?"

Sarah smiled. "My, you're a cute little fellow, aren't you?"

David paused for a moment, parsing her words. "Cute? I know you are, but what am I?"

Sarah laughed. "My name is Sarah."

David paused. "Hi, Sarah! Do you know the magic word?"

"Oh, let's see. Abracadabra?"

After a moment's pause, David opened his mouth and stuck out his pink Plexiglas tongue, making a raspberry noise at Sarah. Sarah and Taliesin both laughed as the gnome slowly wagged a finger at her.

"That's not the magic word!" The gnome turned to Taliesin. "My name's David. What's your name?"

"My name's Taliesin."

After a moment's pause, David's eyes opened wider and his jaw dropped open.

"Taliesin! Do you know the magic word? I'll bet you do!"

Taliesin laughed, leaning in closer to whisper in the gnome's ear.

"Nausicaä."

David paused, parsing Taliesin's response.

"YES!"

The gnome's internal speaker played a short burst of digital fanfare in celebration of Taliesin's correct answer.

Then, he slowly but smoothly leaned forward onto his hands and rose to his feet.

"Follow me!"

David started walking. After a few quick steps, he tumbled from the seat of the park bench. Taliesin gasped in surprise, and Sarah lunged forward reflexively, almost catching David in mid-air. When David landed on the sidewalk, he took a few extra seconds to get back on his feet, then continued walking at a brisk pace for such a small creature.

Sarah and Taliesin followed David down the block. When he reached the corner, he looked both ways, then quickly crossed the street. A young woman walking down the other side of the street stared at the gnome curiously for a few moments, but looked away meekly when Sarah looked in her direction.

Soon, they reached the next corner and crossed the street, walking together for several blocks and making a few turns as the mechanical gnome led them on a circuitous route through the neighborhood. David led them down to the far end of the last block before turning and coming to a stop in front of a dented metal door. It was the door to a rather unremarkable three-story tall brick building with no external signage and plain sheets of plywood covering the few small windows that hadn't been filled in with bricks. David waited a moment for Sarah and Taliesin to catch up, then pressed a small button on the wall that was at just the right height for a gnome his size.

After a few moments, a small speaker next to the door crackled to life.

"Hi there!"

The voice from the intercom sounded remarkably like David's voice. It was feminine, high-pitched, and obviously cheery and boisterous even after speaking only a couple of words.

David looked up at the intercom.

"Hi there! It's me, David."

"Hi, David! Do you have anyone with you?"

"Yes! Taliesin and Sarah. Taliesin knows the password."

"Excellent! Bring them to the Nexus."

The door buzzed and popped open slightly. David stepped forward and started pushing the door open, but he was very small, so the door moved slowly. Sarah chuckled, leaning forward to help David open the door.

"Follow me!"

The interior of the building was lit by a series of fluorescent black light bulbs installed in otherwise standard office light fixtures. As David led them down the long narrow hallway, the bright colors of his clothing became a bit more muted, but his cotton beard was an almost iridescent white. There were several doors on either side of the hallway, some of which were closed, others of which opened into dark rooms with vague silhouettes of furniture, boxes, and irregularly-shaped objects barely visible in the shadows. The walls were painted with occasional smiley faces, hearts, stars, and mathematical symbols that glowed in bright primary colors in the ultraviolet light.

The hallway led to a freight elevator. David stepped into the elevator and waited for Sarah and Taliesin to enter. Once they stepped across the threshold, he stepped forward and pressed one of the three small buttons at his height on the wall of the elevator. The elevator's metal grating door slid shut, and the elevator lurched to life.

Taliesin looked at David with a smile, then looked back up at Sarah.

"I wonder why she doesn't just have him talk to the door and the elevator wirelessly? Wouldn't that save him the trouble of pressing buttons?"

Sarah chuckled. "But where's the fun in that? He looks more like a real little man this way. I like it."

The elevator stopped at the third floor. The metal grating doors clattered and opened, revealing the contents of the top story of the building.

It was a large open room, a hundred feet by fifty feet, unbroken by walls or other barriers. The entire space was lit by a single massive full-spectrum LED bulb that dangled from the twenty-foot ceiling and shone like a brilliant electronic sun. The windows were covered with large flat screen monitors displaying lifelike videos of a lush green forested mountain landscape. The left side of the room had a wooden bunk bed, a long marble counter with wooden cabinets, a toilet, and a small shower stall with transparent glass doors and sides. The right side was home to several metal tables covered with various types of computer equipment, several dozen server towers, and a long metal cabinet filled with loose gears, a mismatched jumble of robotic limbs, circuit boards, wires, and other miscellaneous electronic supplies. The middle of the room was occupied by eight simple metal computer desks arranged in a circle, with a large flat-screen monitor and computer tower on each desk.

A woman in her early twenties stood in the center of the circle. She was short, just barely five feet tall, and her long blond hair floated freely in thin wisps across her cheeks and shoulders. She wore a bright yellow T-shirt, flowing green and purple skirt, and a tablet computer strapped to a rainbow-colored armband on her right wrist. The speakers attached to each of the computers were playing loud electronic music. For a few moments, the woman was oblivious to their presence, dancing in place slightly and singing along to the music as she tapped away at the computer on her arm, glancing up occasionally at the desktop computer in front of her. Then, when David started walking toward her, she spun around to face them, and her brilliant blue eyes opened wide, her lips spreading into a broad grin.

"TALIESIN!"

She pushed a button on her tablet, bringing the music down to a quiet hum. Then, she ran across the room and leapt at Taliesin, wrapping her arms and legs around him and squeezing him tightly. Taliesin laughed, stumbling for a moment to regain his balance, hugging her back as his face flushed slightly.

"Hi, Patricia."

"It's really you! Here you are in analog form!"

Patricia let go of Taliesin, dropping back down to her feet. Sarah noticed that her voice was identical to David's.

"And you must be Sarah!"

Patricia hugged Sarah more gently and tentatively than she had hugged Taliesin.

"Ooh, you're soft! Especially your boobs!"

Taliesin laughed nervously. Sarah grinned, returning the hug and patting Patricia on the back.

"I'm not sure what to say to that. Thanks?"

"You're welcome."

Patricia let go of Sarah, then ran over to David, picking him up and giving him a big hug.

"You made it back!"

"Yes." David's voice was slightly muffled as Patricia held him close to her heart. "I found Taliesin. Taliesin knows the password."

"Excellent. This was your best mission yet!"

Patricia walked over to the nearest desk and set David on the desktop next to a tiny gnome-sized reclining armchair. David leaned forward slightly, then leaned back to plop down comfortably into the seat of his chair. As David started reclining, Sarah noticed a little metal ladder leading from the desktop down to the smooth wooden floor.

"Welcome to the Nexus!"

Patricia led them into the center of the circle. As Sarah looked around at the many computers, she noticed that each one was turned on and was running one or more programs.

"This is where the magic happens!"

Patricia twirled around in place at the center of the circle, her wispy blond hair trailing behind her as she swept her arms in front of the computers. Then, she went around the circle more slowly, pointing to each computer one by one.

"This one's for surveillance, and these three are for research, and these three are for Internet, and this one's for fun!"

Sarah examined the computers curiously, shaking her head with a smile. Taliesin stepped into the center of the circle and looked around slowly, wide-eyed and slack-jawed.

"What... how... Patricia, I didn't even know! This is amazing!"

Patricia grinned.

"Thank you! I do what I can." She walked over to a mini-fridge sitting next to one of the computers. "Soda? Juice? Chips? Granola bars?"

"Sure." Taliesin nodded. "I'll take a soda."

"I'll have a juice."

"Okay!"

Patricia opened the fridge, tossing a soda to Taliesin and a bottle of juice to Sarah. As Sarah noticed a trash can and trash chute on the far side of the room, a thought occurred to her.

"Hey Patricia, when was the last time you went outside?"

"You mean outside outside?" Patricia giggled. "Who knows! Oh, I know who knows." She looked down at her tablet and started tapping away on the smooth surface with her free left hand. "Oh, let's see. Seven months, four days, and six hours ago. That was the first time I took David out to play. That was fun!"

Taliesin and Sarah looked at each other, their eyes widening in surprise and concern. After a moment of silence, Sarah chuckled, looking back to Patricia.

"It's a good thing you have these nice digital windows then."

"Yes!" Patricia ran over to one of the large flat screens, leaning her cheek against it as she rubbed it affectionately. "We're in the Andes right now! Have you ever been to the Andes? The Nexus picks up real-time video feeds from over 100 countries. We can go anywhere in the world!"

With a few taps on her tablet, the windows all faded to black, and the speakers rose in volume for a moment with the distinctive haunting melodies of theremin music. Then, the windows faded back in, revealing a sprawling cityscape as viewed from the top of a nearby mountain.

Sarah sipped at her juice, walking over to look out a few different windows. Between the high quality of the video and the positioning of the monitors, it really did seem as though the building had been transported to a distant location. Sarah leaned in close to one of the monitors, then peeked behind it to reassure herself that it was an illusion. The window behind the monitor was covered with a wooden board similar to the ones she had seen on the outside of the building.

"So you and Taliesin know each other from online?"

"Yes!" Patricia ran over to Taliesin and hugged him again. "He was asking about AR on a public forum! Silly Taliesin, trying to get himself disappeared. And then he said he'd visit me sometime, but he never did! Not until today. I was looking forward to going outside with you!"

"Sorry about that." Taliesin shrugged. "I rarely make it up to St. Louis. Too much work, not enough money."

"So what's AR?"

"Anomalous Revolution!" Patricia's eyes widened. "Oh, you still don't know about it, do you?"

"Taliesin's told me a little."

"There's so much to learn!"

Patricia started tapping on her tablet. The computer monitors in the inner circle started filling with images of people of various ages, genders, and ethnicities. Some were posing for individual or group photos, smiling for the camera with their families and loved ones. Others seemed to be demonstrating extraordinary abilities — a woman levitating above a small crowd, a man with electricity crackling between his outstretched palms, a small smiling child bending an iron bar with her bare hands. One of the monitors showed an elaborate timeline, scrolling through various slides with a long rainbow-colored horizontal line on a black background accompanied by various annotations and photos.

"Like all species, *Homo sapiens sapiens* is constantly evolving. Some silly people out there want to control the evolutionary process, suppressing new developments until they are a 'stable' and 'productive' part of the human genome. Anyone with extraordinary abilities is labeled either a 'Prodigy' or an 'Anomaly'. Prodigies are studied and rewarded. Anomalies are suppressed and disappeared."

Patricia tapped on her tablet. The photos were replaced for a moment with a large red letter A inside of a thick red circle. Then, the symbol faded, replaced with photos of protesters clashing with the police and military of various cities and countries, computer servers similar to those in Patricia's Nexus, and various charts and graphs with photos and fine print that Sarah couldn't take in at a glance.

"Anomalous Revolution has always existed in some form. We are the free thinkers, the ones who dare to live free and actualize the creative evolutionary potentials that are emerging through us. We embrace the label Anomalous because we will never conform to their false Order. We find our own order in our own liberation."

Patricia started looking around at her own slide show as it displayed on the various monitors, her eyes wide with wonder. Sarah and Taliesin looked on with her in silence for a few moments, then Sarah spoke.

"I know a lot of activists. I'm surprised I haven't run into Anomalous Revolution before."

"Oh, sure you have, silly!" Patricia giggled. "We have to be very secretive, even more secretive than other radical activists. But if you know any anarchists, or hackers, or earth liberators, or monkeywrenchers, you probably know one of us."

"I know a few of those." Sarah smirked. "Speaking of which, what are your thoughts on climate change?"

"Oh, climate change!" Patricia spun around and walked over to one of her research computers. "Taliesin told me about that. It's good timing, actually. I've been doing climate research for the past two months!"

Sarah's eyes widened a bit, her lips spreading into a broad smile.

"Seriously?"

"Yes!"

Patricia tapped on her tablet. The monitors on the two research computers started displaying a series of complex graphs and charts, and the rest of the monitors went blank.

"Climatology isn't quite as fun as physics. Too many

variables and all of these weird random equations that I haven't been able to integrate into string theory yet. But I'm starting to get the hang of it, and the computers do most of the work. And there's so much data!"

"What does the data say?"

"The data doesn't say anything; you have to look at it!" Patricia giggled. "Really, though, it's true. Data just sits there looking pretty. What you really want to look at are the models and how accurately they match and predict the data." Her expression suddenly turned grim. "And my models aren't very happy at all. Nope nope. They indicate that anthropogenic climate change has already altered global climate patterns significantly. Even if we stop releasing greenhouse gases today, temperatures and oceans will continue to rise dramatically for decades, and a lot of really sad and scary things will happen. I haven't constructed the necessary economic and sociological models yet to extrapolate the effects this will have on human societies, but I bet there are disastrous consequences when a lot of big cities get flooded by the ocean and burned by wildfires and smashed by hurricanes and tornadoes!"

Patricia stepped up to Sarah, clasping her hands in front of her chest and looking up to Sarah expectantly.

"But you've come to fix it? Taliesin said you've come to fix it. I really, really want to fix it too!"

Sarah smiled, shaking her head with a sigh.

"I've been trying to fix it for years now. Maybe the three of us can make more progress together."

"Yay!" Patricia started bouncing in place slightly. "Are we going on an adventure? I haven't gone on an adventure since I created the Nexus! Did you come in a car? I want to go for a ride in the Mobile Nexus! It's supposed to be for emergencies, but climate change is an emergency, right?"

Before Sarah could respond, Patricia ran over to her sleeping area. She picked up a yellow messenger bag, slung it over her shoulder, and returned to the inner circle.

"I packed when Taliesin texted me. Let's go!"

Sarah laughed.

"We don't even know where we're going yet. We need to get out of St. Louis though. They know we're here. Do you have any AR connections within a few hours of here who can give us a place to stay for the night?"

"Oh, we don't need a place to stay. We can all sleep together in the back of the Mobile Nexus in a big cuddle puddle!"

Sarah smirked. "Sounds good to me. What do you say, Taliesin?"

Taliesin chuckled, looking down at his feet with a grin. "Um, sure."

Sarah patted Taliesin on the back. "Yeah, I didn't think you'd mind. Now, we need a destination. Patricia, do you have any contacts in Chicago?"

"Oh, definitely." She started typing on her tablet. "Chicago's not a hot spot or anything, but they've got millions of people. I know people, and they know people. There's a guy there who can magnetize anything. I had him magnetize a marshmallow for me."

Sarah laughed. "Seriously?"

"Yes! I'd show you, but I ate it." She grinned. "Probably a bad idea, but it was delicious!"

"I'm sure it was." She turned to Taliesin. "How does Chicago sound?"

Taliesin shrugged. "You're the boss."

"Boss?" Sarah laughed. "I'd rather be a team player."

Patricia chimed in.

"Well, you get to be the team captain!"

Sarah smiled, shaking her head.

"Alright, whatever. Anyway, Patricia, what is the Mobile Nexus? Is it a van or something?"

"Oh, it's more than a van." She grinned and giggled, hopping in place excitedly. "Let me show you!"

Patricia ran past Sarah and Taliesin, stepping into the elevator. Just as they started following her, her eyes grew wide with surprise.

"I almost forgot!"

She ran back into the inner circle of computers and ran over to David. After petting him on the head affectionately, she leaned in close and spoke softly.

"I'm going outside for a little while, David."

David looked up at her, pausing a moment as he parsed her words.

"You're going outside?"

David responded in a voice nearly identical to Patricia's, a fact which left Sarah mildly amused and moderately unnerved. Patricia nodded, petting David on the head again.

"Yes, David. You're in charge of the Nexus until I get back."

David paused, then nodded slowly.

"I understand. When my batteries are done charging, I'll be ready to maintain the Nexus. I've had a busy day!"

Patricia giggled. "Yes, you have! Goodbye, David."

She kissed David on the forehead.

"Goodbye, Patricia."

He patted her gently on the nose, then leaned back in his small recliner on the desk and closed his eye shutters.

Patricia gave David one last pat on the head and looked up to Taliesin and Sarah.

"Okay, let's go!"

She ran into the elevator again, and Sarah and Taliesin followed her. Once they were in, she pressed a button on the wall, and they returned to the ground floor.

"This way!"

Patricia led them down a side hallway and into a large loading dock. She tapped on her tablet, activating several banks of bright fluorescent lights that were hanging from the ceiling.

The loading dock was largely empty. The right and far sides of the room were lined with several rows of bare metal shelving units, most of which were empty. A few shelves here and there had a mix of boxes, automotive parts, and unidentified electronic components in various states of repair. The left side of the room had a loading dock with a several foot drop and a stretch of bare concrete leading up to a pair of metal garage doors.

A black minivan was parked in the loading area at the edge of the dock. At first, Sarah didn't notice anything unusual about the minivan, aside from the fact that it was very new and expensive-looking. As she looked more closely, she noticed that the top of the vehicle was covered in a thin sheet of solar panels, and a small black satellite dish was sticking up out of the center of the roof. A thick black cable was lying on the ground near the back end of the vehicle.

"Electric?"

"Oh, of course!" Patricia ran across the room and jumped off of the dock, landing on her feet and petting the minivan affectionately. "This is the Mobile Nexus. It gets a thousand miles per charge, and the satellite uplink has enough bandwidth to run a whole ISP!"

"A thousand miles? That's impossible." She hopped off of the dock, peeking in the slightly tinted windows. "I've been researching and promoting electric vehicles for years now. You'd have to fill the whole cab with batteries to get that kind of range. We're years away from anything near that. How is that possible?"

Patricia grinned, placing a finger over her lips.

"Shhhhh!"

Taliesin walked down the steps at the end of the dock and stood next to the car with Patricia and Sarah. He stood on his toes, studying the solar panels and satellite dish carefully.

"Impressive. I'm guessing you designed this?"

"Oh, not the whole thing, silly. That would be boring. I just explained a few things about electrical engineering to a friend of mine at Tesla Motors. They gave me the Mobile Nexus for free!"

Sarah nodded. "That works." She looked back and forth between Patricia and Taliesin. "Are we ready?"

"Ready!"

Patricia rushed to the driver's side door and hopped inside.

"I call shotgun."

Sarah started walking around to the passenger side door. Taliesin shrugged and got into the back of the van. Patricia tapped on her tablet, turning off the overhead lights and activating one of the large metal doors. The door slid up slowly, clattering audibly as an unseen motor pulled it open. Patricia turned the key in the ignition, and instead of hearing an engine hum to life, they were treated to the sound of a chorus singing a few notes over the minivan's internal speakers. Then, the motor sprang to life with a slight hum, and the Mobile Nexus slid out of the loading dock and onto the street.

CHAPTER 6

*"In visions and dreams
the course of change is revealed.
Nothing is certain."*
— *Bertram Muhnugin, The Death of Birth*

    The full moon emerged from behind the buildings overhead, its silver glow all but lost in the glare of countless fluorescent office lights, street lights, and illuminated signs. Squat stone and brick buildings lurked among the steel and glass towers that stretched impossibly high into the sky above, blotting out most of the stars with their height and light. Traffic hummed, buzzed, and honked in the distance, but the nearest blocks were free of cars.
    Sarah walked down the sidewalk at a brisk pace, rounding the corner of the large stone building and continuing toward her destination. Her left upper arm was bound with a blood-soaked blue T-shirt, covering a wound that filled her bicep with sharp pain.
    As she reached the corner, Sarah saw a lone figure in the distance. He was standing on the corner at the base of the tallest tower in the city, looking around casually as he waited for the light to change. He was wearing a black rubber body suit with a red logo on the chest and a black mask over his eyes. His hair flowed freely over his broad

shoulders, and his gait and stance exuded an effortless confidence and strength without pretense or vanity.

Suddenly, the man's posture tensed, and he turned and looked directly at her. He looked down at her arm, then looked both ways before bursting across the street in her direction at a dead run. In the span of a few heartbeats, he stood before her, a large cloth bandage in one hand, his other hand outstretched toward her wounded arm. His eyes were a clear sky blue, and he looked to her with warmth and genuine concern.

"May I have a look?"

CHAPTER 7

*"A self-made hero
born beneath the tall tower
surrenders to change."*
— Bertram Muhnugin, The Death of Birth

Sarah awoke with a start. It took her a moment to remember where she was and who was with her. As she opened her eyes, she remembered that she was in the back of the Mobile Nexus in the parking lot of a rest stop. Taliesin was cuddling at her side, his arm over her belly and his face buried in her long black hair. Patricia was cuddling along Taliesin's back, her arm wrapped around his chest and her small feet intertwined with his gangly legs. It had been a warm night, so at some point, they had pushed the blanket aside and were lying together uncovered.

Sarah slowly slipped out from underneath Taliesin's arm, doing her best not to disturb his slumber. He stirred slightly, then settled back into stillness as she slid open the side door of the minivan.

It was a cool morning in early May in central Illinois. At the other end of the parking lot sat a small brick building with a wooden shingle roof and two glass doors on either side of a floor-to-ceiling glass wall. Inside the rest stop, there were vending machines, maps, and restrooms.

Outside, there was a concrete sidewalk, a stretch of short grass, and a patch of woods. The parking lot was mostly empty, populated by a sparse mix of semi trucks and a handful of cars and SUVs. Beyond the parking lot was the highway, with four lanes of traffic zipping by at high speeds. The air was filled with a discordant mix of the smell of car exhaust and the scent of morning dew in the grass.

Sarah stood a few feet away from the minivan for several minutes, watching in silence as the traffic passed by. She thought about her dream, and the prophecy of the High Priestess, and the fact that only a day and a half ago, she had apparently used psychokinesis to stop an oncoming vehicle from killing her. Now, she was traveling cross-country with two virtual strangers, destination unknown, running from trouble and hoping to solve the global climate crisis that she'd spent her entire adult life working on.

What did it all mean?

As she stared at the tree line at the edge of the highway, her thoughts calmed, and she settled into a deep meditative silence. The treetops swayed slowly, waves of wind rustling the leafy green canopy. When she focused her attention on the trees, she could hear the sound of the wind rustling through the leaves, in spite of the constant buzz of the highway. As the leaves rustled against one another, she could almost feel the touch of leaf against leaf, with thousands of leaves and branches dancing together slowly in the wind.

After a few minutes, she heard the sound of voices coming from the minivan. Taliesin's quiet, even tone almost blended into the background noise, but Patricia's bubbly high-pitched voice rose above the morning silence. For a moment, the speed and volume of Taliesin's voice rose to match Patricia's as the two talked to each other excitedly. Then, the minivan door slid open, and Patricia hopped out onto the blacktop, followed soon after by Taliesin.

Patricia stepped up to Sarah, stopping less than arm's length away from her.

"Good morning!"

She waved to Sarah with a big smile, looking up at her expectantly. Sarah returned the smile with a light chuckle.

"Good morning, Patricia."

"So what's the plan?"

"Plan?" Sarah smirked. "There's a plan?"

"Sure there is!"

Patricia started tapping on the tablet computer on her wrist. She had taken it off while she was sleeping and used it as a pillow. Now, it was once again attached to her wrist by two simple straps.

"Our best bet is my friend Addy's house. We're still going to Chicago, right? There's a whole AR neighborhood in the suburbs, but we should go for something more underground. My friend Addy has a few friends with a bungalow that nobody else knows about. Nobody but me!"

"Sounds good." Sarah looked over at the rest stop. "Let's use the restrooms and get back on the road."

Patricia and Taliesin went into the rest stop while Sarah looked back at the view. After a few minutes, they returned to the vehicle. The three travelers got back into the Mobile Nexus and headed out onto the road.

The rest of the trip to Chicago went by quickly. As Patricia drove, she talked at great length about a variety of scientific and philosophical topics: quantum physics, electrical engineering, organic chemistry, climatology, sociology, psychology, and her theories about the underlying nature of reality and the prospects for a Theory of Everything to unite all of the sciences. Taliesin occasionally asked her questions and Sarah mostly listened, speaking up suddenly whenever climatology came up and asking detailed questions about current climate research and models. Whenever Patricia launched into a detailed discussion of the mathematical formulae involved, Sarah and Taliesin both fell silent, and Patricia eventually switched back to a discussion of general principles. Before they knew it, they were passing through the far southern suburbs on the highway, making their way into the city.

As they rode into the city, the Chicago skyline rose into view on the horizon. Even though they were still out in the far suburbs, the Sears Tower was clearly visible from a distance, looming high above the rest of the city. Numerous other towers of steel and glass rose alongside it at varying intervals, most of them dwarfed by the height of what had once been the tallest skyscraper in the world. They were arriving around lunchtime, which was not nearly as slow and congested as the morning or evening rush hour, but still left them surrounded by seemingly endless streams of vehicles flowing in and out of the city. Some of the suburbs had erected long sound walls along the edge of the highway to mute the constant hum of traffic, leaving little more than treetops visible from behind the walls. Soon, however, they found themselves within the city limits, surrounded by chain link fences, overpasses, and taller buildings of brick, concrete, and steel.

"So my friend Addy lives on the North Side." Patricia glanced down at her tablet. "We should be there in... hey, wait a minute. Is one of you thinking about the Sears Tower?"

Sarah's eyes widened.

"Yes. How did you know that?"

"My map is trying to lead us to the Sears Tower!" Patricia giggled. "Have you been talking to Tabby? I didn't know you could talk to computers too!"

Sarah shook her head. "I didn't know either. Not a big computer person."

Patricia took her eyes off the road for a moment to shoot a wary glance at Sarah in the back seat, wagging a finger in her direction.

"I've got my eye on you!"

Patricia returned her attention to driving. Taliesin turned around in his seat to face Sarah.

"Okay, two things. First of all, it's called Willis Tower now, not Sears Tower. Second, you have psychokinesis and computer telepathy? That's weird."

"Weird?" Sarah laughed loudly, punching the back of Taliesin's seat. "And here I thought it was normal!"

Taliesin chuckled. "Okay, that came out wrong. But I'm serious. Most Anomalies only have one anomalous ability, or two related abilities, like healing and hurting people. But psychokinesis and computer telepathy? It doesn't make any sense."

"I think I can see the future too."

"Oooh!" Patricia turned back toward Sarah. "What's in my future?"

Sarah pointed out the front windshield. "Eyes on the road."

"Aww, okay."

Sarah explained the dream she'd had the night before. Taliesin listened, nodding as she told the story. By the end, his face was more serious and his features more ashen.

"Any idea what happened to you? And where were we at?"

"I don't know." She paused. "I'm sure you two were fine. It felt like you two were together somewhere safe, but I don't know where. Frankly, I was more concerned about running into whoever had shot me. At least I think it was a gunshot wound. I've been teargassed and beaten with a baton, but never shot before, so I'm not sure what it feels like. It could have been a stab wound."

"Well, the future can change, Sarah. Even what clairvoyants see can change. I hope we can keep you safe." His ashen features flushed a bit as his lips upturned in a warm smile. "And if you do get shot, don't go wandering around the streets of Chicago without me! Let me heal you."

Sarah chuckled. "Alright, sounds like a plan. Let's really be careful about meeting up with this friend of yours, though. Where are we meeting her?"

"Portage Park. It's a great big park on the north side. It has a lot of trees and big open space, and it's not far from her house, and we're almost there!"

For the next few minutes, they rode together in silence. The streets were lined with an irregular mix of concrete and brick storefronts and small apartment buildings. Soon, they pulled into a parking lot and got out of the Mobile Nexus to examine their surroundings.

Portage Park was a public green space that was several blocks long on either side. From the lot, Sarah could see several baseball fields, a moderate canopy of trees, and a large curved stone wall on the corner. The wall marked the main entrance to the park, with a broad opening and a wide concrete path that led through the trees and grass that covered most of the park.

For a moment, Sarah smiled warmly at the sight of what almost amounted to a patch of woods in the middle of a major city. As soon as they started walking toward the park, though, her heart started racing, and she froze in place.

Patricia had already rushed up to the nearest tree and started climbing it. Taliesin was about to follow her when he felt a twinge of panic and turned to notice Sarah standing motionless near the Mobile Nexus.

"Sarah? Is everything alright?"

Vague, urgent impressions swirled through her mind, and she was unable to focus. She felt physically ill and unable to move, her heart racing and her breath shallow. She had never had a panic attack before, but she suspected she was having one now.

"No."

Taliesin walked over to her and put a hand on the side of her shoulder. For a moment, his eyes widened and he withdrew his hand in shock. Then, he took a deep breath, focused his attention, and placed his hand on her shoulder again. After a few moments, her breath and heart rate started returning to normal. She snapped out of her dazed state, taking Taliesin's hands in her palms and relaxing with a slow sigh.

"I don't usually panic like that, but I just had some sort of vision." She looked at the park and shook her head, taking a step back. "We can't go in there. We'll all die if we go in there."

"What?" Patricia hopped out of the tree and hurried over to Sarah. "Should I call Addy?"

"No." Sarah shook her head. "We have to go."

Taliesin and Patricia looked at each other, then looked

back at Sarah.

"Okay. But I at least have to text her."

Patricia started typing on her tablet, pacing back and forth a bit as she typed. Taliesin let go of one of Sarah's hands but held the other one firmly in his palm as they both scanned the edge of the park for signs of trouble.

"Do you know what's going to happen? Is there something we should be looking for?"

Sarah spun around suddenly and pointed at a group of four people standing in the distance. The first two were a young man and woman dressed in casual T-shirts and jeans, holding hands and looking anxiously into each other's eyes. The other two were a man in his twenties and a woman in her thirties, both dressed in black suits, both glaring sternly at the younger couple.

For a moment, from a distance, it didn't look like there was a problem. But then the young woman's expression turned from anxiety to anger, and she started poking the man in the suit with her index finger, yelling angrily.

"How dare you threaten my child! If you people come after me one more time, I swear to God I will kill you all!"

The pair in suits took several steps back, raising their hands up in a gesture of surrender. The woman in casual clothes took a step forward, shrugging off the restraining hands of her lover as she continued pointing and yelling at the man in the suit.

"Did they even tell you what I can do? You have no idea how patient I've been with you people! I—"

Suddenly, she was hit in the back by a long black tranquilizer dart. As she slumped to the ground, her partner caught her, his eyes wide in shock.

"NO!"

The young man's shout exploded through the park like a clap of thunder. For a moment, time seemed to stand still as everyone in the park turned to look for the source of the sound. Then, Patricia recognized the face of the woman as her lover laid her down on the pavement.

"Addy!"

Patricia burst forward at a dead run toward her fallen friend. Sarah and Taliesin looked at each other for a moment, then Sarah pointed to Taliesin.

"Stay!"

Taliesin froze in place, clenching his fists slightly and leaning forward as if ready to run. Sarah broke into a sprint after Patricia. She was a slightly faster runner, but the distance was short, and Patricia had a head start.

As soon as they had taken a few steps in Addy's direction, a tranquilizer dart hit the young man crouching next to Addy. Instead of collapsing, he let loose a primal scream as his entire body was bathed in sparks of electricity. The man and woman in suits both reached down and drew their weapons, but before either could get off a shot, the young man extended his palms toward them, blasting them with crackling bolts of electricity. They were lifted off their feet for a moment, jerking and spasming in mid-air as their unconscious bodies slammed limply into the concrete.

By this point, Patricia had almost reached the scene, with Sarah still several yards behind her. Suddenly, several shots rang out in rapid succession, and the body of the electrified man jerked and twisted at uncomfortable angles. The bolts of electricity enveloping the man crackled out of existence, and his broken body fell lifelessly against the pavement.

"No!"

Patricia shouted and clenched her fists, stopping next to the prone figure of her friend Addy and turning her attention to an unmarked white delivery van that had pulled up on the sidewalk a few dozen yards away. There were two people clad from head to toe in black body armor pointing assault rifles at her, and several more pouring out of the unmarked van. In addition to the usual riot gear, each of them had thick goggles and large headphones covering their ears.

Patricia shot an angry glare at the people with the rifles.

"Leave her alone!"

Patricia reached down and started dragging her friend Addy away. Several more shots rang out, and Patricia jerked to the side sharply, spinning around and slamming face first into the concrete.

Sarah stopped just short of Patricia, turning to face the shooters with a steely glare and a guttural growl. By now, all six of the blackclad figures had emerged from the van and raised their weapons. Their assault rifles were all pointed at Sarah. As they opened fire, however, an unseen force deflected their fire in mid air, sending a hail of bullets ricocheting back in their general direction. All six of them jerked and twisted with the force of multiple impacts, dropping their weapons as they lurched backward against the van behind them. Five of them fell to the ground, and the sixth one managed to stay on his feet as he slammed against the van and held onto it for support. He was clearly, however, barely able to stand.

Sarah stared at them blankly for a moment, stunned by her own continued survival. Then, she grabbed the back of Patricia's shirt and started dragging her off of the concrete and onto the grass in the general direction of the Mobile Nexus.

When Sarah was halfway back to the Mobile Nexus, several more shots rang out. These shots were slower and more irregularly paced than the others. Sarah glanced up to see that the last of the blackclad shooters left standing had drawn a handgun and was taking slow, careful shots at her. One of the bullets tore a chunk out of the inside of Sarah's left bicep, grazing her torso and nicking one of her ribs. Another one grazed her right ear, cutting through the cartilage and leaving her right ear ringing. The other eight were near misses, whipping through the air around her and slamming explosively into the trunks of surrounding trees.

As the shooter reloaded, Taliesin rushed forward, helping Sarah lift Patricia into the van. On any other day, Sarah could have lifted Patricia by herself without difficulty, but flexing her left arm sent white-hot pain shooting through her bicep, nearly causing her to let go of Patricia's legs entirely. She felt the patch of hot wet blood on her arm spreading as she and Taliesin slid Patricia into the back seat. Sarah climbed into the driver's seat and Taliesin climbed into the back with Patricia. Bullets started pelting the van, but the windows were bulletproof, cracking heavily but not shattering as three more shots hit the windows and four more hit the sides. After what seemed like an eternity, they pulled away from the curb, and Portage Park receded into the distance.

As they sped down Irving Park Road, Sarah kept glancing in the rear-view window, looking to see if they were being followed. So far, no one seemed to be following them. She glanced in the mirror again to see Taliesin holding Patricia in his arms, his hands applying pressure to a gunshot wound on her leg, his eyes closed and his lips moving silently as he mouthed the words to a prayer.

"You alright back there?"

Taliesin finished his prayer before responding. "I think I can stop her bleeding." He shook his head, his voice trembling. "I've never treated a gunshot wound before, but I think her bleeding is slowing down. If I can stop her bleeding, I think I can heal her."

"You can definitely heal her. I have faith in you. Just stay calm and focused. You can do it."

Sarah glanced at the floor of the passenger side and saw Patricia's bag. When they came to a red light, she reached down and pulled a T-shirt out of the bag, tying it around her left bicep as best as she could. She used her teeth to pull the knot taut. Then, as the car behind them started honking, she noticed that the light was green and continued driving.

The two windows that had been hit by bullets were side windows. Sarah used the controls on the driver's side door to roll these windows down. One of them stuck at the halfway point as the damaged glass became caught in the door, but Taliesin reached over and nudged it with his elbow a few times, allowing the window to slide down into the door.

For several minutes, the three drove together in silence. Patricia was unconscious, but her bleeding was slowing to a trickle. Sarah and Taliesin were both ashen and shaken, with Taliesin staring down at Patricia while Sarah stared blankly ahead at the road. Eventually, it was

Taliesin who spoke.

"The bleeding stopped."

"Oh. Good."

"Are you okay?"

"I'm not going to bleed out, if that's what you mean."

Taliesin paused. "How did you do that?"

"You mean deflect those bullets?" Sarah laughed suddenly, her hands gripping the wheel. "Hell if I know. I just glared at them with every ounce of rage I had in my body. I assumed I was going to die, honestly. But I wasn't about to be shot in the back."

They drove aimlessly for several more minutes, with Sarah making random turns every few blocks to see if anyone was following them. Once she was fairly sure that they weren't being tailed, she started looking for a good place to pull over.

"I'm sorry, Tal."

"Sorry?" Taliesin looked at her reflection in the review mirror. "Sarah, this wasn't your fault."

Sarah shook her head. "I should have seen it coming. I knew something bad was going to happen, but in the dream, I wasn't worried about you, so—"

"Clairvoyants can't see everything, Sarah. And I know we joked about you being the boss, but you're not in this alone. We're all in this together."

"Thanks."

After a few more minutes of driving, Sarah turned at the entrance to a large parking lot in front of a grocery store. They pulled into a parking space near the back of the lot.

Sarah turned off the engine. For a few moments, she continued staring at the road, and they sat together in silence. Then, she got out of the driver's side of the vehicle and walked around to the side door, opening it up and climbing in with Taliesin and Patricia.

"How is she?"

Taliesin looked down at Patricia. The metallic scent of fresh blood hung heavy in the air. Most of Patricia's shirt and part of her right leg were soaked in it. She was laid out in the back seat with Taliesin kneeling in the space between the two middle seats of the van. Taliesin had found the first aid kit and bandaged Patricia's leg. He was currently applying pressure to the bandages covering a gunshot wound to her abdomen.

"She's stopped bleeding. Can you help me bandage this?"

Sarah took some medical tape out of the first aid kit and helped Taliesin apply clean bandages over the bloody ones. When they were done, Taliesin continued staring at Patricia for a few long moments, then leaned against one of the seats beside him with a sigh.

"I've never seen anything like this."

He looked down at his blood-soaked hands, trembling slightly at the sight of them. He glanced at Patricia, then looked to Sarah.

"I think I can heal her, but it will take time. I usually heal sprained wrists, the common cold, normal things. This is insane."

"You can do it." She put a hand on Taliesin's shoulder, rubbing his arm warmly. "I'll stay with you until she's conscious."

Taliesin stared blankly into the distance for a moment, then snapped to attention, looking at Sarah's bloody arm.

"Your arm! Here, let me bandage that."

"We're out."

"Already? I thought we still had—"

"I remember the dream. I'm sure you don't have any more bandages."

Taliesin rummaged through the first aid kit and looked around on the floor, nodding slowly.

"I guess you're right. Are you okay?"

Sarah chuckled, a slight grin on her lips and a dark glimmer in her eye. "Yeah, this is nothing. You should see the other guy."

Taliesin laughed nervously, touching her wound lightly. She wasn't sure if it was intentional or simply reflexive, but she felt a healing warmth flowing from Taliesin's hand into her wound.

"When I'm done with Patricia, I'll heal you too."

She smiled, brushing aside his hand and placing it on

the bandaged wound on Patricia's abdomen.

"No, you won't."

Taliesin looked at her curiously, his eyes filled with concern. "What do you mean?"

"As soon as Patricia's awake, we need to split up. I need to find this guy at the Sears Tower while you finish healing her."

"Oh, no." Taliesin shook his head, taking his hands off of Patricia for a moment as his face flushed with anger. "No you don't. We are not splitting up. I don't care what dreams you had or what—"

Sarah leaned forward and turned Taliesin to face her, kissing him suddenly on the lips. After a moment's surprise, he returned the kiss, reaching to run his fingers softly down her unwounded arm. They both relaxed, and for a moment they pulled closer together, moving toward each other a bit awkwardly in the cramped space in the back of the van. Then, Sarah pulled back slightly and looked at Taliesin with a smile.

"It's going to be alright. It's not going to be easy, but it's going to be alright. I'm going to find this guy, and we're going to get back on the road and figure out what to do."

Taliesin sighed, nodding with a slight smile.

"Alright. As soon as you find him though, you have to come back. I don't want to be alone right now."

She reached out and put her hand over Taliesin's heart, feeling his heart as a healing warmth passed between them.

"You're not alone."

She held her hand over his heart for several moments, looking into his eyes as she continued.

"I'll stay with you until Patricia wakes up, and then I'll be back as soon as I can."

"Alright."

The two looked into each other's eyes for another long moment. Eventually, Sarah patted him on the shoulder and grinned.

"Okay then. Let's get back on the road!"

Without another word, she got out of the van, closed

the door, and hopped back into the driver's seat. With a turn of the key, the electric motor hummed almost silently back to life, and they were back on the road.

    Sarah decided that staying on the move was better than staying still. She started driving aimlessly, weaving in and out of the side streets while generally heading away from the site of the shooting. For a few minutes, Taliesin sang his healing song as he laid his hands on Patricia's wounds, but eventually the singing grew quieter and tapered off as he slipped into a silent trance. They drove around in silence for an hour or two before she stopped at a drive-thru fast food chain to buy them snacks and drinks. Taliesin was in deep concentration, focusing his entire attention on healing Patricia, but Sarah convinced him to take a quick break for long enough to eat and drink something. Then, they were back on the road, driving aimlessly south and west through the suburbs for several hours before heading back into the city.

    As dusk fell over Chicago, the sun disappeared behind the buildings to the west, casting the skyline in a reddish orange glow. The lights of the city started turning on, bathing the passing cars and pedestrians in artificial luminescence as the sky slowly slipped into twilight. Traffic was heavy on Lake Shore Drive as they drove north past the traditional stone columns and modern angular walls of Soldier Field. To the east, Lake Michigan stretched off into the distance as far as the eye could see, its shore lined with a bike path and wide stretches of grass and trees. To the west, there were several large fields with trees that obscured most of the shorter buildings from sight. Soon, they passed by a large park with an elaborate water fountain that Sarah recognized as a landmark she'd seen on TV often and visited once as a child. After passing the park, they turned left on Jackson, heading straight toward the Sears Tower.

    "Ow."

    The soft sound of Patricia's scratchy voice filled Sarah with a sudden surge of joy followed by a soft sigh of relief. She could almost feel a similar response from Taliesin even though she didn't turn around to see him as he stirred from his trance and spoke to Patricia.

"Patricia! Welcome back."

"Did I get shot?"

"Yes, you did."

"That was awful! Suddenly I couldn't breathe or think, and everything hurt, and everything went black. But then you healed me! You healed me, right?"

"Yes, I did."

"Thank you! Ow."

Sarah glanced in the rear view window to see Patricia attempting to sit up and Taliesin placing a hand on her shoulder, coaxing her into laying back down.

"Not yet, not yet! Lay down for a little while longer, please. You still need more time to heal. You had three gunshot wounds, any one of which would have probably killed you under normal circumstances. You may not be back to normal again for days."

"Normal? I'll never be normal!"

Taliesin and Sarah both laughed. Sarah turned onto a side street and started looking for a parking spot. After searching for a few blocks, she found an empty spot and pulled into it. Sarah turned off the engine and leaned back into her seat with a sigh.

"Alright, folks. Time for me to go for a walk."

"But Sarah—"

Sarah raised a hand to interrupt Taliesin.

"No buts. You take care of Patricia, I'll go look for this masked man."

As she opened her door, she turned around in her seat and reached back to Taliesin, clasping his hand in her own for a moment.

"I'll be back soon."

Taliesin's smile was warm, but eyes were filled with concern.

"You'd better be!"

Sarah felt a rush of warm healing energy flowing into her body through Taliesin's hand. She basked in it for a moment, then smiled and let go.

"I will be."

Sarah left the car, closing and locking the door behind her. She had been to Chicago before, but not often enough or recently enough to remember her way around the city. Their parking spot wasn't far from the Sears Tower, though, and she remembered which direction to head in to get there. After glancing around a bit to see if anyone was watching her, she started walking.

The sky was fully dark now, but the lights of the city were shining brightly, leaving the night sky all but forgotten overhead. For several minutes, Sarah walked in the opposite direction of the Sears Tower, debating whether or not to act differently than she had in the dream. The improvised bandage on her arm attracted one or two strange looks, but she was relieved when her fellow pedestrians didn't ask any questions. They just kept walking, either too busy to care or wary of striking up a conversation with a wounded stranger. Eventually, though, she started looping back toward her destination.

For a moment, the full moon emerged from behind the buildings overhead, its silver glow all but lost in the glare of countless fluorescent office lights, street lights, and illuminated signs. Squat stone and brick buildings lurked among the steel and glass towers that stretched impossibly high into the sky above, blotting out most of the stars with their height and light. Traffic hummed, buzzed, and honked in the distance, but the nearest blocks were free of cars.

Sarah walked down the sidewalk at a brisk pace, rounding the corner of another large stone building and continuing toward her destination. As she recognized which street she was on, her hands clenched into fists reflexively, filling the bullet wound on her left bicep with a renewed flash of sharp pain.

As she reached the next corner, Sarah saw a lone figure in the distance. He was standing on a corner at the base of the tallest tower in the city, looking around casually as he waited for the light to change. He was wearing a black latex body suit with a red logo on the chest and a black mask over his eyes. He also wore a black utility belt. His long golden hair flowed freely over his broad shoulders. His gait and stance exuded an effortless confidence and strength without pretense or vanity.

Suddenly, the man's posture tensed, and he turned and looked directly at her. He looked down at her arm, then looked both ways before bursting across the street toward her at a dead run. In the span of a few heartbeats, he stood before her, a large cloth bandage in one hand, his other hand outstretched toward her wounded arm. His eyes were a clear sky blue and his skin was naturally bronze. He greeted her with a look of concern.

"May I have a look?"

Sarah was tempted to make a snide remark, but she found his genuine warmth and care disarming.

"Yes."

She extended her arm so that he could examine her wound. He removed the tied-on T-shirt, wrapping the wound tightly with a fresh bandage.

"This looks serious. Is this a gunshot wound? You need to see a doctor."

Sarah smiled. "If I see a doctor, they'll probably dissect me. Luckily, I've got a healer on my side. I'll be fine."

The man looked at her quizzically. "Healer?"

"Yes. At first, I didn't believe it either, but—"

"Don't worry, I believe you." He paused for a moment, scanning the area to see if anyone was standing nearby. "I'm on my way to meet up with a few friends. Care to join me?"

"Sure."

They started walking at a brisk pace in the direction that the man had come from. After taking a few steps, he stopped and turned to face her, extending his hand to shake hers.

"My name is Hart."

She glanced down at the large red logo on the chest of his body armor. It was the outline of the head and horns of a deer with a small black heart in the center of its forehead.

"Hart like the deer?"

Hart smiled broadly.

"Yes. Usually, I have to explain what a hart is."

Sarah grinned.

"I've seen a hart in the wild. I know one when I see one."

"I'm the only Hart I've seen so far." He smiled broadly. "What's your name?"

"Sarah."

"Pleased to meet you, Sarah."

"Pleased to meet you too, Hart."

The two walked together in silence for several minutes. Sarah enjoyed the slightly cool night air in spite of the fact that it carried with it the unwelcome scents of car exhaust and motor oil. Every once in a while, they caught a glimpse of the moon to the east, though it was barely noticeable amidst the harsh glare of street lamps and the fluorescent lights of surrounding buildings. At one point, someone in a passing sedan honked and waved at Hart, shouting their approval as they drove by. Hart waved back with a nod and a smile.

"Do you get that a lot?"

Hart chuckled. "Most of the responses are positive. Some people laugh at me, but I don't mind. Every once in a while, someone picks a fight."

"How does that work out for you?"

Hart smiled. "Better than it works out for them."

Sarah laughed. "So you do you do this often? Patrol the streets of Chicago dressed as a superhero?"

Hart nodded. "I have a day job, but this is my life's work. And I'm not alone. There are half a dozen of us here in Chicago and hundreds across the country and around the world. Some of us go on neighborhood watch patrols. Others work with local charities. I do a bit of everything."

"It makes sense. I'm an environmental activist from Southern Illinois. I've worn a bear costume before, but never a superhero costume."

Hart laughed heartily. "It's not for everyone. But it works for me."

The two walked together in silence for several more minutes until they reached a large park. As they started walking down the path into the park, they heard a voice cry out in the distance.

"Hart!"

A young man dressed in bright red and blue spandex waved and started jogging in their direction. He was tall and gangly, with short black hair, blue eyes, and a big smile on his smooth teenage face. He wore a thin blue mask over his eyes and a black utility belt similar to Hart's around his waist. Several other people in costumes were standing at a roundabout in the park path and started walking toward Hart and Sarah. They met the newcomers halfway, and the man in red and blue looked to Hart and Sarah expectantly.

"So who's the new girl? Is she a mask?"

"Girl?" Sarah laughed. "I'm a woman. How old are you, sixteen?"

"Pfft. Eighteen. No minors on the Guard. Too many complications."

Hart stepped forward, waving his hands to present Sarah to the group.

"Friends, this is Sarah. Sarah, these are members of the Windy City Guardians."

"Hi Sarah. I'm Go, short for Chicago, spirit of a city on the move. This is Silver Spider, Black and Blue, Haymarket, Pythia, and Dauntless."

Silver Spider was a short, wiry man who wore a black and silver spandex costume that was clearly inspired by a more famous spider-themed superhero. Instead of a mask, however, he wore goggles and a bandanna over his pale face and buzz-cut hair.

Black and Blue was a tall, lanky young man with dark brown skin, short hair, a thick mustache, and a low-key costume consisting of black cargo pants, a lightweight blue jacket, and a black shirt with a black and blue Yin Yang symbol.

Haymarket was a young man with short brown hair, black combat boots, black cargo pants, a black flack jacket, and a black headband with a red letter A inscribed in a red circle. Everyone else's expression was warm and welcoming, but Haymarket's expression was cool and somewhat wary, studying her carefully to determine her intentions.

Pythia was a middle-aged woman with greying black hair, olive skin, a flowing white tunic, tight leather pants, a black messenger bag, a tablet computer in her hand, and tall black boots. When introduced to Sarah, she bowed slightly and smiled with a mischievous twinkle in her eyes.

Dauntless was a tall, muscular man in his mid-twenties. He had short blond hair, blue eyes, and square features. He wore black combat boots, grey camouflage pants, and a black shirt with a silver star inscribed in a golden circle. Sarah also noticed that he was wearing a large camping backpack that sagged slightly with the weight of a full load.

After the introductions were complete, Go turned back to Sarah.

"So who are you? And what's up with the arm? Did you guys get into a fight?"

Hart smiled, shaking his head. "It's alright, Go. She's a friend. Let's just start the patrol."

He turned back toward the direction they'd come from and motioned for everyone to follow. Sarah walked alongside him as the rest of the group followed close behind, spreading out to fill the entire sidewalk.

As they walked together, Go spoke quickly and steadily, prodding Sarah for information and sharing an endless stream of trivia about the Windy City Guardians and the city they served. For the first few minutes, he spoke mostly with Sarah, then started speaking with the rest of the team just as eagerly. He was by far the most talkative, but Haymarket and Dauntless had a brief side conversation about politics, and Black and Blue told everyone the latest news about a community garden project he had started this year. Pythia quietly typed and tapped and swiped on her tablet computer, and Silver Spider kept glancing at Sarah but looking away with a smile when she met his gaze.

At one point, when Go was at the back of the group talking to Haymarket, Sarah turned to Hart and whispered in his ear.

"Is he always this talkative?"

Hart chuckled. "He means well. They find him annoying sometimes, but he keeps their spirits up."

Sarah texted Taliesin to let him know that she was fine and would be gone a while. She patrolled with the group for several hours, walking through a few parks and wandering along busy streets and side streets in search of trouble. They encountered several enthusiastic fans, a handful of hecklers, and several dozen people who looked like they may be living on the streets. Some of them called out to Hart or Go from a distance, while others were sitting or standing quietly and seemed wary of the group at first. Hart and Go spoke to each of them briefly, and a few at greater length, offering bottles of water, prepackaged food, clean socks, and toiletries, all of which Go retrieved from the large pack that Dauntless carried on his back. A few turned them down, but most were quietly thankful, and one elderly woman was openly emotional, thanking them profusely in broken English for their kindness.

"We're glad to be of service, ma'am." Hart shook her hand, patting her on the shoulder affectionately. "Be safe, and be well."

After walking for a few more minutes, they stopped outside of an Irish pub so that Silver Spider could use the restroom. Sarah checked to see if she had missed any texts from Taliesin. While Go was busy explaining the history of pubs and the origins of the word "pub", Hart pulled Sarah aside and stepped just out of earshot of the rest of the group.

"You mentioned a healer." He scanned his surroundings, seeing if anyone was listening and lowering his voice before continuing. "Are you Anomalous? Are you part of the AR?"

Sarah shrugged. "I didn't know about AR until yesterday, but I'm definitely Anomalous. I'd look like Swiss cheese right now if I weren't."

Hart leaned in closer to her, putting a hand on her shoulder as he whispered to her. "I got into this line of work because someone shot me. In the chest. When I woke up a few hours later, my shirt was soaked in blood, but my heart was beating and my chest and lungs were rebuilding themselves. I can't heal other people, but I naturally heal from things that would kill most people."

Sarah nodded. "I was nearly hit by a car. I stopped it with my mind. I also deflected some bullets with my mind." She smiled, rubbing her wounded bicep idly and noticing that the pain had diminished.

"The only one who knows about my power is Pythia. Haymarket suspects it. I don't think he has any powers, but he's very political. He's an AR supporter."

Sarah paused, considering her words carefully before continuing.

"Hart, I hate to ask this, but I need you to come away with me and my friends. I've had a prophetic vision, and I'm looking for a self-made hero beneath the tall tower. You must be the man I'm looking for."

Hart's eyes widened. "Self-made hero beneath the tall tower? That's what Pythia called me when she met me."

By this point, Silver Spider had rejoined the group, and Go was walking up to Hart and Sarah.

"Alright guys, let's 'Go'!"

Hart held up a hand to halt Go.

"I..." He trailed off, looking back and forth between Sarah and the group. "I need to go do something."

Pythia slid her tablet computer into her messenger bag. She stepped forward, placing a hand on Hart's chest.

"I know."

She looked to Sarah with a knowing smile and a glimmer in her deep brown eyes.

"You're her, aren't you? Daughter of the flame, born in the Heartland, looking for a self-made hero beneath the tall tower?"

Sarah chuckled, her face flushing with a mix of self-consciousness and amusement.

"Yes, I suppose I am."

Pythia fell to one knee at Sarah's feet, bowing her head in reverence.

"You have important work to do together, milady.

Take good care of him."

Pythia rose to her feet. The others looked on in bemusement, looking back and forth in wonder at Pythia, Hart, and Sarah. Hart's normally calm and confident demeanor wavered as he held his hands out awkwardly in mid-thought, searching for words and looking off into the distance.

"I need to think this over. Sarah, walk with me."

He turned away from the group and started walking toward the corner. Before Sarah could follow, he paused, facing the group one last time.

"This could take until morning, so I may as well say goodbye for the night. Go, stick to the green patrol routes until I get back. Everyone, I look forward to seeing you again soon. Namaste."

He placed his palms together in front of his heart and bowed deeply, then started walking and motioned for Sarah to follow.

Sarah turned back to the group.

"Goodbye, everyone. Nice meeting you."

Go shook her hand. "Likewise!"

Pythia stepped forward and hugged her, bowing again slightly as she stepped back. "Blessings on your journey."

Silver Spider, Black and Blue, Dauntless, and Haymarket all waved as she left. Sarah waved back, smiling at Silver Spider as he stole another quick glance before looking away bashfully. By this point, Hart was rounding the corner, so Sarah hurried to catch up with him.

The two walked together in silence for a few moments before Hart spoke.

"I need to pray for guidance."

"Pray?"

"Yes. I used to live at a homeless shelter called Interfaith House. While I was there, I met a priest from Old St. Patrick's Church. I've prayed there ever since."

"Alright, let's go."

Hart shook his head. "They're not open at this hour. I'll have to go in the morning. Can you meet me at the corner of Adams and Des Plaines at 11 a.m.?"

"Sure."

"Good." He stopped in place, turning to Sarah to shake her hand with a broad smile. "It's been a pleasure meeting you! I look forward to seeing you again tomorrow."

Sarah returned the handshake. "Yes, I'll see you then."

For a moment, their hands lingered together. Hart smiled broadly, his clear blue eyes shining from behind his black mask. Sarah's pulse quickened as she returned the smile, taken aback by his quiet confidence and unabashed affection. Soon, the moment passed, and he placed his hands palms together in front of his heart, bowing deeply to her before turning and walking away.

The walk back to Taliesin and Patricia took over half an hour. Along the way, she passed dozens of unfamiliar faces. Few of them noticed her and none of them spoke to her. As she wound her way back to the Mobile Nexus, her mind fell silent as she absorbed the sights, sounds, and smells of the big city. In the quiet moments, she listened to wind whistling between the tall steel towers, ran her fingers along the worn stone and brick buildings, sniffed the scent of car exhaust and fine cuisine, and felt the electric hum of a living city crackling in the air around her. It had a cold, metallic taste to it, devoid of the moist, heavy scent of soil and leaves that brought Sarah such comfort on her long hikes through the forests of Southern Illinois. But the city of Chicago had a life of its own, a bustling energy of bright lights and dazzling sights that left her feeling like she'd had too much coffee and not enough hours in a lifetime to take it all in.

Before she knew it, she found herself standing alongside the Mobile Nexus. Taliesin and Patricia were both asleep in the backseat, with Taliesin holding Patricia in his arms and resting his cheek on the top of her head. Sarah smiled as she saw them and quietly slipped into the driver's seat, locking the door behind her. At first, she didn't feel tired, and wondered idly if she might stay awake until it was time to meet Hart in the morning. But as soon as she closed her eyes, she drifted off to sleep.

CHAPTER 8

*"In the sacred groves
and in the churches of man
they will sing for change."*
— *Bertram Muhnugin, The Death of Birth*

"There he is!"

The Mobile Nexus was parked in the parking lot kitty-corner from Old St. Patrick's Church. Sarah was sitting in the front seat and Taliesin and Patricia were sitting side by side in the back. Patricia was pointing at Hart as he walked toward the church. She bounced excitedly in her seat, tapping Sarah on the shoulder and pointing again.

"See, there he is! I've read about Real Life Superheroes but never seen one in person! Some of them don't have good costumes, but that one looks like someone out of a movie!"

Taliesin chuckled. "Yes, he does."

"Okay, you two wait here. I'll introduce you to him when he decides to come with us."

Taliesin looked out the window, studying the approaching figure carefully as he started walking up the church steps.

"What if he doesn't come with us?"

Sarah smirked. "Trust me, I've got this."

She opened the door and slid out of the Mobile Nexus,

closing the door behind her and leaving the parking lot.

Old St. Patrick's Church was a beautiful building, humble in size but rich in dignity. As Sarah approached the church, she felt a reverence for it that caught her entirely by surprise. The old beige bricks and stone foundation were heavy with the weight of over 150 years of history. Sarah's mind was flooded with a series of images that felt like memories but were entirely new to her — an early glimpse of the church before either of its green spires had been built; a room full of young women in uniforms studying together in a classroom; a full congregation in old-fashioned clothes gathered for mass; a vision of her own mother in her youth, her belly slightly round with her only child, praying for guidance on the fate of a daughter conceived out of wedlock.

Sarah snapped back to the present moment and realized that she had slowed to a stop on the steps of Old St. Patrick's. For a moment, she stared blankly at the large Celtic cross on the main doors of the church, debating whether she should wait outside for Hart or go inside. Before she had made a conscious decision, she found herself stepping forward and walking inside.

As she crossed the threshold, Sarah felt a sense of wonder that she had only experienced before in the heart of the forest. She took several gradual steps forward, running her hand along the smooth edge of the stone font at the center of the entryway, staring in wonder at the life-size statute of St. Patrick and his shamrocks, the ornately carved stonework, the stone altar, the bright light of Spring filtering in through the intricate artwork of the stained glass windows. There was a stained glass skylight over the altar itself, and the sun was close enough to high noon that the skylight bathed the statues and altar in warm radiance.

Sarah stopped next to the font, soaking in every detail of the old church. Hart was in one of the pews near the front, his head bowed and hands folded in prayer. An elderly couple sat a few pews behind him, and across the aisle, over a dozen girls were clustered near three women in nun's habits. Some of the girls were praying quietly while others were reading and occasionally whispering to each other.

As Sarah looked at the girls, they suddenly all rose to their feet and turned to face her. Her heart started racing, and for a moment she was startled by their seemingly unprompted and perfectly synchronized behavior. But each of the girls had a warm, tender smile on her face, as if she had each just seen her long-lost mother walk into the room.

The three nuns looked on curiously, whispering to each other as the girls stepped into the aisle and started walking in a single file line toward Sarah. She placed her hands on the cool stone in front of her while the girls formed a circle around her. As she looked down into the water of the font, the girls joined hand and started to sing.

"Gabhaim molta Brigidhe!"
"Gabhaim molta Brigidhe!"
"Gabhaim molta Brigidhe!"

The words were unfamiliar to her conscious mind, but their meaning resonated through every cell of her body and every corner of her being. The full lyrics of the old Irish hymn devoted to St. Brigid sprang into Sarah's mind like a forgotten memory, but the girls repeated the introductory line of praise to her.

"Gabhaim molta Brigidhe!"
"Gabhaim molta Brigidhe!"
"Gabhaim molta Brigidhe!"

As Sarah stared into the water, she realized that she could see more than she had seen a moment before. She could see the entire interior of the church from all angles — Hart rising to his feet and standing in the aisle; the three nuns standing behind him; the stained glass of the triptych windows on the wall behind the balcony overhead. She could see the church from above and below, with the Mobile Nexus in a nearby parking lot. She could see the whole city from a distance, a dizzying rush of countless minute details. She could feel channels of causality coursing through her and around her in all directions, connecting her to her past, her future, the lives of those around her. She felt a surge of brilliant light within herself, filling her with indescribable currents of joy and sorrow. She knew with absolute certainty that taking dramatic public action at this time would catalyze the change that she sought. Once she knew this, her attention returned back to the channels of causality, back to the city as seen from a distance, back to the church she was standing in, and back to the font of water before her.

"Gabhaim molta Brigidhe!"
"Gabhaim molta Brigidhe!"
"Gabhaim molta Brigidhe!"

As Sarah came back to her waking consciousness, the girls fell silent. After a few moments, they all suddenly burst into laughter. The laughter broke their trance, and they turned to each other and Sarah with a mix of quizzical looks, smiles, blushes, and laughter. Soon, they scattered from the circle one by one, scurrying back to the nuns at the other end of the church.

Sarah stood there for a moment in stunned silence. When Hart walked forward and caught her eye, she looked up to him and smiled warmly.

"That was beautiful."

It wasn't until Sarah noticed the surprised look on Hart's face that she realized that they had said the words simultaneously. They both laughed, and this time it was Hart who spoke.

"I don't know what you saw, but I know what I saw." He placed a gentle hand on her shoulder. "I will go with you wherever your journey takes you."

"Thank you. And for once in my life, I know exactly where I'm headed. Let's go!"

Sarah took Hart by the hand and led him out into the street. As they walked toward the Mobile Nexus, Patricia and Taliesin got out of the vehicle and started walking toward them. Taliesin walked at an even pace, but Patricia rushed excitedly forward.

"Superhero! A Real Life Superhero!" Patricia giggled, stopping in front of Hart and bouncing up and down in place. "My name's Patricia. What's your name?"

Hart smiled warmly. "My name's Hart."

"Ooh, Hart like the deer!" She tapped on the tablet on her wrist, pulling up information on him. "There you are. Wow, you're famous. And here you are in analog reality!"

Patricia suddenly gave Hart a big hug. He was over a foot taller than her, so her head only reached his chest level. He returned the hug, then turned to Taliesin.

"Hi, my name's Hart."

"I'm Taliesin. Pleased to meet you."

As the two men shook hands, Sarah clasped her hands together in front of her heart and faced the group with a mischievous grin.

"Alright, folks. I have good news and bad news."

Taliesin studied Sarah's features carefully.

"Have you had a vision?"

"Yes! That's the good news. I've had a vision, and I know exactly what we need to do, and Hart here is coming with us."

"Yay!" Patricia hugged Hart again. "We get to keep him!"

Taliesin looked at Sarah, waiting for the other shoe to drop.

"And the bad news?"

"We're going to St. Louis — and we're going to get arrested."

Patricia's eyes widened and jaw dropped. The color slowly drained from Taliesin's face. Hart crossed his arms, the smile fading from his lips. The silence hung in the air between them for several long moments before Hart spoke.

"You're sure about this?"

"Yes."

"Then let's go."

Hart walked over to the Mobile Nexus and got in the passenger seat. Sarah grinned, following Hart and motioning for Taliesin and Patricia to follow her. After looking at each other for another moment, they caught up to Sarah and got into the back seat of the van. Sarah slid into the driver's seat, turned on the Mobile Nexus, and pulled out into the street.

CHAPTER 9

*"Charming magician
weaves a web of deception.
Change must fall to rise."
— Bertram Muhnugin, The Death of Birth*

"I still don't get it."

The Mobile Nexus crawled along I-55 through the dense rush hour traffic heading into St. Louis. Patricia was asleep in the back with her feet on the seat beside her and her head resting on Taliesin's lap. Hart was in the passenger seat eating an apple and reading a book. Sarah was at the wheel, gaining some time by darting between the cars with exceptional precision while also analyzing the numerous possible outcomes of their trip to St. Louis. Without losing focus on her driving and planning, she mulled over Taliesin's comment and responded without skipping a beat.

"I don't fully get it either." She snatched Hart's apple out of his hand, took a big bite, and handed it back to him, flashing him a quick smile in the process. "But something's going to be different this time."

"So the International Prometheus Consortium is a think tank?"

"Yes. They're heavily funded by the oil and coal industries. And they're very effective. If you see a story on

PEN News about climate change, or oil, or anything related to energy, it's taken verbatim from an IPC white paper. IPC comes up with all sorts of dirty little schemes to raise doubt about climate change and praise oil drilling, 'clean coal', and natural gas as the solutions to all of our problems."

"I hate PEN News." Taliesin shook his head. "All of the big ones are bad, but PEN is the worst."

"Definitely."

For a few moments, they drove on in silent agreement. Soon, however, Taliesin remembered his original point.

"But you've been there before. You've protested before. You've even been arrested before, right?"

"Yes. About a dozen of us blockaded the entrance with a banner and demanded that they stop spreading lies about climate change." Sarah smirked. "It wasn't all that effective, but we did get a good article in the St. Louis Post-Dispatch."

"So what's different this time?"

Sarah paused, thinking back to her vision, trying to remember what it felt like to be connected to all of those channels of causality flowing in every direction to places she had been or would be, people she had met or would meet, choices she had made or would soon be making.

"Everything. I can't put my finger on it, but everything feels different now. I feel different. Traveling with the five of you feels different. And something about IPC headquarters feels very different today."

Taliesin gave her a curious look. "You mean traveling with the three of us?"

"Yes., three. What did I say, five? Anyway, if we get arrested there today, it'll make national news, maybe even global news. And they won't just be talking about the arrest. They'll be talking about climate change."

The four drove together in silence for several minutes. The weather had been mostly sunny on the drive in, but now the sky over St. Louis was completely overcast. As Sarah pulled into the mall parking lot, the electric scent of the coming storm hung heavy in the air, promising rain before the day was done. She parked in an empty spot near the edge of the lot and turned to face her companions.

"Alright, folks. Let's do this."

Sarah and Hart got out of the Mobile Nexus and waited by the front bumper while Patricia gathered her yellow messenger bag and Taliesin held his pendant and said a quick prayer. Patricia still seemed a bit pale and groggy, but otherwise showed no signs of her recent injuries. When everyone was ready, they crossed the parking lot and started walking down the sidewalk toward their destination.

"We're just a couple of blocks from the IPC." Sarah looked down the street and saw that the side street leading to the IPC was blocked with a few traffic cones and orange wooden sawhorses. "Patricia, you'd better start broadcasting now just in case."

"Yay! I've always wanted to do a live feed!" Patricia pulled out her expensive digital camera and turned it on, tapping on her wrist tablet a bit before pointing it at Sarah. "Okay, go!"

"Ready? Okay."

Patricia hurried forward a few steps to get a better shot of Sarah, Hart, and Taliesin. Sarah clasped her hands together in front of her heart and smiled warmly at the camera.

"Good afternoon, Internet! My name is Sarah Athraigh, and I'm an environmental activist from Gorton, Illinois. I'm in St. Louis today with Hart, Real Life Superhero and our friends Taliesin and Patricia to challenge the lies and misinformation of the International Prometheus Consortium. Patricia's adding some links with documentation of the IPC's lies. In the meantime, we'll be dropping by the IPC unannounced to ask them a few questions about human-caused climate change."

They continued down the street and turned at the blockade, walking past the traffic cones and sawhorses without pausing. There was no one guarding the intersection, but Sarah did notice several men in suits across the street following them at a discrete distance.

There was also a large unmarked black van down the street making a cautious but illegal U-turn to come back toward the IPC. Sarah ignored them for the time being and continued toward their destination..

Prometheus Plaza looked entirely out of place amidst the more traditional storefronts and restaurants of the neighborhood. The plaza spanned an entire city block and featured a smooth stone floor, winding rows of stone pillars that stood several stories tall, and a thirty foot tall stone statue of Prometheus holding a stainless steel torch with a real blue fire that burned brightly beneath the overcast sky. The office building at the center of the plaza dominated the landscape, a steel and glass sculpture that was broad at the base and twirled into a tapered top like the tip of a flame.

Hart, Taliesin, and Patricia all slowed down as they looked in wonder at the large statue and unusual building. Sarah slowed to match their pace. Most of the scene was very familiar to her since she had been to a half dozen demonstrations here over the past couple of years. To her surprise, however, a small temporary stage had been erected in front of the Prometheus statue. Several men and women in suits and ties stood at the podium on the stage, and dozens of reporters and spectators stood at the foot of the stage with cameras, microphones, and several tablet computers, documenting the press conference on stage.

When Sarah saw the man behind the podium, her mild surprise turned into shock and disbelief. Even at a hundred paces, she could recognize that man at a glance. The broad, sweeping gestures he made as he spoke and the smug, self-assured tone of his voice were both unmistakable. Her eyes widened, and her heart started racing in her chest. She froze in place, clenching her fists and searching for her voice for a moment before speaking his name.

"Percival Sword."

Sarah's three companions stopped with her. Patricia's jaw dropped, and Taliesin scrutinized the man on the podium, a look of disbelief slowly spreading across his face.

"No, it couldn't be." Taliesin shook his head. "No, he lives in Wales, doesn't he? He has dual citizenship, but he doesn't actually live here."

"It's him."

Hart looked at the man curiously, then gave Sarah a questioning look.

"Who's Percival Sword?"

Sarah chuckled. The laughter set her at ease, snapping her out of the momentary shock.

"He's the owner of PEN News and the whole PSI Entertainment Network. PSI is Percival Sword Incorporated. He basically turned himself into a corporation and built the world's largest media empire around his big fat ego."

"Oh, that guy." Hart shrugged. "I didn't know his name. I don't like PEN News, but they make good movies."

"Sure, if you like a lot of explosions without any plot."

Sarah glanced at the men who were following them and noticed that they had almost caught up. She looked away and took Hart by the hand.

"Come on, let's go."

Sarah strode boldly toward the podium. Hart walked by her side, and Patricia and Taliesin fell back a few paces to record the action.

Percival Sword was a man of modest stature but powerful presence. He was lean in frame and stood an inch or two below average height, yet his sweeping hand gestures and sheer enthusiasm for speaking empowered him to claim a disproportionate amount of personal space. His short black hair, bold red polo shirt, and black khakis were perfectly crisp and clean, and his brilliant blue eyes twinkled like twin sapphires above his sharp Roman nose and broad thin-lipped smile. As he stood at the center of the stage, all eyes were upon him. He greeted his audience with a radiant warmth and charm that even his detractors found difficult to resist.

"I love this city." Percival beamed at the audience, giving the podium an affectionate tap as he continued.

"The spirit of this city is the spirit of Heartland, USA. It's a spirit of industry, a spirit of hard work and home-grown innovation. And IPC is at the heart of it all. I can think of no better way to celebrate the 150th anniversary of IPC than by paying a visit to the place where it all began — right here in St. Louis!"

The audience applauded enthusiastically. By this point, Sarah and Hart had reached the edge of the crowd and were making their way to the front. Percival drew a long breath and raised his hands as if to continue, but Sarah emerged from the crowd just in time to interrupt him.

"Is denying climate change a part of that spirit of innovation?"

Some of the reporters turned their cameras on Sarah and Hart as they approached the podium, stopping just a few feet short of the edge of the stage. The stage was only three feet tall, so they were very close to Percival now. A burly man in a suit and tie stepped forward and put a protective hand on Percival's shoulder, but Percival smiled and motioned for him to step back. His clear blue eyes studied Sarah quickly but carefully. Somehow, she felt as if he could see into the deepest recesses of her soul, dissecting her every thought with the ease of a master surgeon performing an autopsy.

"Pioneering clean coal and natural gas is part of that spirit of innovation." He returned his attention to the rest of the audience with a smug smile. "But I've already spoken about that to the real reporters. If you want more information for your blog, I can recommend a good news site."

Chuckles and laughter murmured through the audience. Hart crossed his arms over his chest and glared at Percival disapprovingly. Sarah took another step forward, standing within arm's reach of the podium. As Percival's cold blue eyes stared her down, she was surprised to find herself feeling small, quiet, and insignificant.

Suddenly, she felt a rush of warmth and light flowing within her and all around her, snapping her out of her moment of fear and reminding her why she was here. A single ray of sunlight burst through an opening in the clouds overhead, bathing Sarah in its golden radiance.

Everyone fell silent. All eyes were on Sarah as she spoke.

"Global warming is real. Human industry, agriculture, and transportation are the primary cause. Your willful denial of the obvious is destroying millions of human lives and disrupting the balance of all life on this world. If you do not acknowledge this truth right now, the whole world will know you to be a liar."

Everyone stared at Sarah, dumbfounded. For the first time he could remember, Percival found himself with nothing to say. He gestured as if to speak, and flapped his jaw as if to stammer, but no sound emerged. Finally, he lowered his hands and spoke, his brows furrowed in genuine confusion.

"What are you?"

Before Sarah could respond, she felt the sharp sting of something piercing the flesh of her upper back. Hart cried out in shock, flinging himself in front of Sarah as several more tranquilizer darts whistled through the air in her direction. The rest of the darts slammed into Hart, but the damage was already done. As Sarah and Hart tumbled to the ground, arm in arm, the light faded, and Sarah slipped into unconsciousness.

CHAPTER 10

*"Change is in order
and order is in for change.
The architect dreams."
— Bertram Muhnugin, The Death of Birth*

Light.

Sarah stared blankly into the light, unaware of where she was and what was happening. Was this the afterlife? She had always been curious about what fate awaited her consciousness at the point of death, but had never come to any firm conclusions. Wasn't there supposed to be a tunnel with light at the end of it? Maybe she had already walked through the tunnel.

When she blinked, she realized she was still alive.

Turning her head and looking around, she realized that she was in a room of some sort. However, it was unlike any room she had ever been in before. The white ceiling and blue walls glowed with an inner luminescence, bathing the room in a warm light that looked and felt remarkably like daylight. When she tried to move, she discovered that her arms, legs, and torso were held fast by smooth, cool cuffs that felt like they were made of glass or possibly porcelain. The room was small, possibly ten by ten, and she seemed to be alone. However, she felt an unsettling certainty that she was being watched.

"Hello?"

Her voice was a bit scratchy, as if she'd been asleep for a long time. She remembered the incident at Prometheus Plaza and realized that she'd been hit by tranquilizer darts.

For several long moments, there was no response to her cautious greeting. Eventually, however, she heard the soft hiss of a door sliding open and the light squeak and patter of a pair of boots moving across the floor.

"The Preceptor is on his way."

The voice was deep and resonant, but the tone was flat and difficult to read. Sarah stared at the ceiling for a long while, idly wondering what a Preceptor was and where her friends were. Soon, the door hissed again, and a quieter pair of boots entered the room.

"Good morning, Sarah."

The bed she was lying on slowly rotated to an upright position. For a moment, she was left looking at a blank blue wall. Then, the bed rotated horizontally, turning her to face the center of the room.

There were two men standing in the room. One was a tall barrel-chested man dressed from head to toe in black body armor. He was armed with an assault rifle and wore thin black gloves, a black helmet, big black headphones, and thick goggles. The other man was average height with short black hair, sharp blue eyes, pale skin, and a muscular build mostly hidden beneath a crisp uniform of black tactical pants and a white button-up shirt. The most striking aspect of his appearance was a headband made of solid gold with a large diamond Eye of Providence framed in a gold circle looming in the center of his forehead.

Sarah stared at the crown, mesmerized by the Eye of Providence. She had seen a symbol almost exactly like it on the back of a dollar bill before, but it had never really caught her attention before. Now, she felt the unsettling presence of a very real intelligence silently observing her from behind that bold diamond eye.

"It's a nice touch, isn't it?" The Preceptor tapped the side of his headband lightly with his index finger, smiling warmly at Sarah. "You know nothing of our history, yet you already know what this is, don't you? I can see it in your eyes. Most of my staff will never perceive what you have already gleaned at a glance. Excellent."

The Preceptor turned to the wall beside him and held his hand out a few inches away from it. A white circle with a black outline appeared on the wall beneath his palms. With a few strokes of his hands, he accessed the room's security settings. The restraints on Sarah's arms, legs, and body retracted into the bed, leaving her free to slide a down a few inches and land on her feet. She was still a little groggy from the tranquilizers, so she took a moment to steady herself on the surface behind her before placing her full weight on her feet.

The guard looked back and forth between the Preceptor and Sarah, holding his assault rifle tensely at the ready over his chest. The Preceptor waved him off dismissively with a slight smile.

"Don't worry, I'll take it from here." He motioned for Sarah to approach him. "Come with me. We have much to discuss."

For a moment, Sarah simply stared at him quizzically. As he turned around and walked out of the room, she decided to follow.

The hall was similar to the room — white ceiling, blue walls, and green floor, all glowing with a uniform luminescence that was bright enough to illuminate the entire hallways with warm daylight but soft enough that looking at the panels felt comfortable and natural. The Preceptor noticed her studying the walls and paused in place next to her, tapping the nearest wall lightly with his knuckles.

"Transparent ceramics." He smiled broadly. "This technology is so advanced that I had to approve it personally. Our well-armed friend back there could unload his entire clip into this wall without penetrating it. The optical properties, however, would be affected."

They continued down the hall, passing several identical unmarked doors before stopping in front of one near the end of the hall. The Preceptor held his hand up to the door and the white circle appeared, allowing him to open the door with a few quick gestures.

When the door slid open, Sarah's eyes widened. Taliesin, Patricia, and Hart were all sitting in transparent chairs around a transparent table, leaning in close to have a quiet conversation.

"Sarah!"

Patricia ran up and hugged Sarah, squeezing her tightly to the point of mild discomfort. Taliesin and Hart said nothing, but a look of relief washed over both of their faces as they stood up and approached her. Taliesin walked over to join Sarah and Patricia in their hug, but Hart stopped a few feet short, crossing his arms over his chest and quietly glaring at the Preceptor.

"Do I detect hostility and posturing?" The Preceptor smirked, carefully studying Hart's body language and facial expression. "You know, if it were up to the Guardian, you'd all be dead right now. Luckily, Bill's not the Preceptor. Not yet, anyway."

Patricia let go of Sarah and matched Hart's stance, crossing her arms and glaring at the Preceptor, her fist clenching so tightly that she started trembling slightly. "This isn't funny! Are you the boss? Why didn't you kill us? Doesn't the Order like to kill Anomalies? You killed Addy!"

The Preceptor cringed, his head twisting slightly and his lips curling as he drew breath with an audible hiss. "We are not called the Order. We are simply Order. We are currently the most advanced manifestation of Order, the most fundamental principle of reality. And it is through our efforts that humanity has evolved from a squalid mass of feuding peasants to a global empire of information technologists in under two centuries. Come, follow me."

The Preceptor started walking down the hall, motioning for the others to follow him. Hart placed a hand on Sarah's shoulder to stop her from following.

"I don't trust him."

"Oh, I don't either. But we may as well get the full tour. Maybe we'll get to meet Bill."

Sarah started following the Preceptor down the hall.

Taliesin looked to Hart and shrugged, taking Patricia by the hand and walking with her down the hall. Hart shook his head with a sigh and uncrossed his arms, following after them. After turning a corner, they all got into an elevator with the Preceptor.

"Welcome to the Panopticon."

The Preceptor stepped out of the elevator and beckoned for Sarah and her companions to follow. The Panopticon was a spherical room with a hundred foot diameter. The bottom half of the sphere was filled with a series of multicolored transparent ceramic desks of varying shapes and sizes, with one to three people in uniforms similar to the Preceptor's sitting at each desk in a fairly spacious and organic layout. Each desk had one or more flat screen monitors along with occasional personal items such as family photos, paintings, potted plants, and small sculptures. The curved blue dome of the upper half of the room was framed with two tiers of transparent aluminum walkways holding additional desks and personnel. A lone walkway extended out to the center of the room to support a six foot diameter glowing crystal sphere. The sphere was displaying a map of the world, with most of the ocean showing as a pale greenish grey while the land masses were complex blends of various hues, tints, shades, and tones of green, yellow, orange, and red.

Sarah and her companions stepped out of the elevator, looking around in wonder. Several of the people at the desks stared openly at the new arrivals, but when Sarah sought to meet their gaze, they averted their eyes and returned to work. The Preceptor led his guests across the walkway to stand around the large glowing sphere.

"The Eye uses a complex algorithm and vast amounts of data to create a real-time model of the integrity of consensus reality. Green indicates areas where all is going according to plan. Red indicates deviation. This includes satellite detection of Anomalous activity, meta-analysis of media and surveillance reports, and so on."

Sarah studied the globe carefully. Most of the land

masses were various shades of green. Major cities were criss-crossed with patches of green, yellow, and orange. Several whole nations were more yellow than the rest of the map, and each continent had hundreds of small splotches of red scattered across its face like so many blemishes.

"You have no idea how hard we work to keep this globe green. Every time Anomalous activity goes public somewhere, that region turns red. Every time a technological advance is made ahead of schedule, that region turns red. Sometimes a whole city turns red and we don't even know why. If we can't contain it, and it spreads, then consensus reality collapses, and the world as we know it ends."

Sarah crossed her arms over her chest, studying the globe carefully.

"Let me get this straight. Every time someone, somewhere, does something that you didn't plan on, a red dot appears on this map?"

"Well, not every time, but yes." He tapped on one of the red dots. "This little pocket of deviant consciousness has the potential to rewrite the whole consensus in its image. Maybe it's a political or religious faction that wants to take over the world. Maybe it's an invention that will destabilize the economy. Maybe it's some teenager who's using the power of his mind to burn down his school. Whatever it is, it is Anomalous. And we must contain and neutralize Anomalies. We must restore Order before consensus reality corrupts beyond repair or dissolves entirely."

Sarah stepped up to the Preceptor, standing only a few inches away from him, her face twisting in anger.

"No. I don't buy it. I get it, but I don't buy it. Where's the freedom in your little plan? What if we like being freaks and thinking outside the box? What gives you the right to enforce your rigid blueprint on a living, breathing reality? The only thing more more amazing than your technology is your arrogance."

"Typical." The Preceptor smirked. "You people and your Anomalous Revolution. When architects design better bridges, you praise their ingenuity. When we design better societies, you condemn our hubris."

"Architects don't murder people."

The Preceptor's lips tightened and nostrils flared in anger. For several moments, he simply glared at Sarah in silence. Eventually, he spoke.

"Everyone dies, Sarah. I make sure they die in the right order."

Sarah and her companions stared at the Preceptor in stunned silence. Before any of them could regain their composure, the Preceptor's expression brightened again.

"I have an idea! Let's go on a field trip! When it's over, you're free to go."

The Preceptor walked past Sarah and headed toward the elevator, gesturing for the others to follow him. They looked to each other with mixed looks of confusion and hope. As the others started walking toward the elevator, Hart crossed his arms and stood his ground.

"What's the catch?"

The Preceptor paused next to the open elevator door. "Catch? There's no catch. Just listen to the rest of my story. Once you do, you're free to go."

Sarah, Taliesin, and Patricia followed the Preceptor into the elevator. Hart sighed, shaking his head and walking slowly down the walkway to join them.

The entrance to the Museum of Real Faery Tales consisted of two large oak doors with wrought iron hinges and thick iron rings for handles. Above the door, there was a roughly hewn oak sign with iron letters that read "MUSEUM OF REAL FAERY TALES." The doors looked entirely out of place at the end of the glowing transparent ceramic hallway, to the point that Sarah stared at them for a while to make sure that they weren't some sort of painting or projection. When they reached the doors, the Preceptor pulled on one of the handles, opened the door, and stepped inside, gesturing for the others to follow.

The Museum of Real Faery Tales was a bit larger than a football field, with a thirty foot high ceiling and a cobblestone path that wound up and down dozens of aisles of various different types of displays. Some consisted of large touch screens that showed interactive slide shows or films. Others featured life-sized wax figures in period clothing ranging from medieval armor to Renaissance formal wear to modern business suits and black body armor.

The Preceptor started leading the group down one of the aisles, narrating as they walked.

"Since the dawn of history, human beings have encountered strange phenomena that defy all rational explanation. People lost in the woods encounter misshapen creatures that look almost human, but not quite. Ghosts of the dead haunt abandoned buildings or pay visits to the living. Wild-eyed madmen drink vials of toxic reagents or recite arcane incantations to develop supernatural powers over space and time, matter and energy. "

The Preceptor stopped in front of the largest diorama in the museum. A dozen immense men, large even by modern standards, were clad head to toe in shining steel armor and adorned in flowing black tabards, each with a bold white circle on the chest. Most of the men were wielding massive two-handed longswords. Two were armed with long, thin blades in one hand and a tower shield strapped to the other arm. An average-sized man was fully armored but had not drawn any weapons, instead reading from a book and shouting angrily at their opponent.

Their opponent was by far the most striking part of the diorama. It looked somewhat like a naked human being, but the proportions were all wrong. It was almost twenty feet tall, and though it was currently hunched over to engage in combat with the men, it was still large enough to make them look like toddlers by comparison. Its ruddy green skin was thick and leathery, and its hairy arms were abnormally long, bulging with thick veiny muscles uncharacteristic of such elongated features. Its eyes, nose, and mouth were all disproportionately large, giving its blood-smeared face a crowded and inhuman look. Its eyes literally glowed with a crimson inner light, and its distended jaw was clenched around the helmeted head that it had just pulled loose from the body of one of the human combatants that it held in its massive long-fingered hands. A stream of blood was squirting from the space where the man's head used to be, forever immortalized in motionless crimson wax that glistened wetly as though it were the real thing.

"Cool!"

Patricia looked up at the monster with a big smile and eyes wide with wonder. Sarah, Taliesin, and Hart looked up at it with more somber expressions but no less a sense of awe. As they studied the creature, the Preceptor continued.

"This is real. This is why we must maintain Order. The Horror of Wiltshire killed all of those men, and it would have ravaged all of England if a second band of Order initiates hadn't finished it off while it was still wounded."

Taliesin studied the statue of the creature.

"Is this a troll?"

"It was an unknown Faery creature. When it shambled into town and started devouring children, no one thought to ask its name."

"Surely it must have had a reason. Did someone destroy its habitat?"

The Preceptor laughed.

"Oh, there's always a reason. But does the reason make sense to a sane human mind? I've read your profile, Taliesin. I know that you communicate with Faeries during your rituals. You should know better than your friends here how dangerous some of these creatures are."

He paused for a moment, looking up at the Horror of Wiltshire with a cold, angry glare.

"They are Anomalous. Their psychology is alien, and they have the ability to warp reality itself with nothing more than the power of their minds. They're among the most dangerous Anomalies in the world."

"So what does any of this have to do with us?" Sarah turned away from the huge statue to face the Preceptor. "Are you saying I'm one of these creatures?"

The Preceptor laughed. "No. You're a human female

with as-yet-unidentified Anomalous qualities. I'd love to see you in one of my labs someday. In the meantime, this is just a warning. Don't be seduced by the simplistic romanticism of Anomalous Revolution."

"What about the simplistic tyranny of Order? You—"

The Preceptor cringed, his head twisting slightly as he held out a hand to interrupt Sarah. "Order is complex, not simple. And Order is aristocracy, not tyranny. We are the best and brightest of humanity united in the service of the evolution of human consciousness. We do not simply hunt human Anomalies like animals. We study them, we learn from them, and we declare some of them Prodigies who are expanding the boundaries of human potential."

"And what's the difference between a Prodigy and an Anomaly?"

"We have a rigorous protocol to determine the difference. But truthfully?" He reached into his pocket and pulled out a shiny gold pen. "This is the difference. The Sovereign and the Council of Order have entrusted the Preceptor with the duty of determining what is and is not a part of consensus reality. If I believe that humanity can handle the presence of an Anomaly without destroying itself or devolving into mass insanity, I will declare it to be a part of the consensus. This is true of both Anomalous human beings and Anomalous phenomena."

"So have you declared us part of the consensus? Or are you going to neutralize us too?"

"In this case, it's not that simple. Sarah, walk with me for a moment. Patricia, why don't you and your friends go find the Anomalous technology exhibit."

"Ooh!" Patricia's eyes widened. "I knew there'd be a forbidden tech display! Is there a wax figure of Nikola Tesla? Let's go see!"

Patricia grabbed Taliesin and Hart's hands and started leading them away. Hart resisted at first, eying the Preceptor suspiciously. Sarah shrugged, and the Preceptor smiled.

"Don't worry, noble knight. I'll bring her back in one piece." He turned to Sarah, leaning in closer and lowering his voice. "He's a bit overbearing, isn't he? Not letting the womenfolk out of his sight?"

Hart glared silently at the Preceptor. Sarah smiled at Hart, catching his eyes and softening his expression with a warm look.

"I find it endearing." She touched Hart lightly on the shoulder. "I'll be fine, though, Hart. I'll be right back"

Hart sighed, shaking his head in resignation. Patricia tugged on his hand again and started pulling him down another aisle. Once Sarah and the Preceptor were alone, they started walking in a different direction.

"Do you know why I've brought you here, Sarah?"

"Climate change?"

The Preceptor smiled broadly. "I knew you were bright, Sarah. You're often quiet, but not for want of insight or lack of communication skills. You're constantly listening, watching, feeling — mindfully perceiving the situation with all senses and analyzing it from all angles. Yet you act with the intuitive spontaneity of a dancer or martial artist. With experience and training, you could join Order."

Sarah laughed. "Is that a compliment or an insult?"

"An observation."

The Preceptor stopped next to a large blank portion of the wall. He held his hand near the wall until a black circle appeared, allowing him to enter a few commands and pull up a window with an image of a globe similar to the one that they had seen in the Panopticon.

"Order is much more tenuous than most realize. The more sophisticated our models become, the more clear it becomes that climate change is an insurmountable crisis."

The Preceptor tapped a button on the screen, and a counter showing the current year appeared next to the globe. As the counter started advancing through the years, the colors on the globe fluctuated smoothly. After a couple of decades, the fluctuations became more sporadic. Around 2050, the entire globe flashed crimson and quickly faded to black.

"Too much is happening too quickly. Floods, droughts, wildfires, rising oceans, increasing frequency and severity of storms. Climate disasters displace tens of millions, which in turn leads to global instability, which in turn hastens human output of greenhouse gases."

The Preceptor tapped the screen again. The computer started displaying scenario after scenario, each of them ending in similar flashes of crimson and black.

"I've tried everything. If we use force to stop all fossil fuel use today, the world quickly descends into violence and madness. If we don't, climate disasters worsen, ultimately forcing a global collapse. If we accelerate technological development, we're torn apart by Anomalies old and new. If we simply neutralize the majority of humanity, the climate recovers briefly, but the survivors are quickly torn apart by various psychological, social, and supernatural Anomalies. In short, consensus reality as we know it depends on a steady supply of cheap oil, but can't withstand the consequences of consuming it."

Scenario after scenario played out on the screen in front of them. For a long time, the two of them stared at the pulsing, flashing globe in silence. Eventually, Sarah was the first to speak.

"So you want us to do something about climate change?"

"Yes."

Sarah laughed. The Preceptor's smooth demeanor faltered for a moment, gawking at her slack-jawed as if she had suddenly gone insane.

"This isn't funny."

"No," Sarah's expression suddenly sank from amused to somber. "It's not funny. I just have a dark sense of humor. First a goddess tells me to do something about climate change. Then the head of some fascist global conspiracy tells me to do something about climate change. What's next, aliens?"

"Fascist?" The Preceptor cringed, clenching his fists for a moment before resuming his commanding composure. "One of my predecessors personally led the effort to neutralize the Nazi Anomaly. I realize the moral dilemmas inherent in my line of work, Sarah, but we are not fascists."

"Then what are you?" She pointed at the glowing globe displayed on the wall. "This is all well and good, but you know that I won't work for you, right? That I would never work for someone who blackbags or assassinates everyone who disagrees with their little plan for a New World Order?"

The Preceptor smirked. "Oh, yes, I know. It's all right here."

With a few quick gestures, the Preceptor pulled up a new display that featured a photo of Sarah accompanied by several paragraphs of text. He scrolled through the profile to display more photos of Sarah and paragraph after paragraph of detailed analysis, including a timeline of her life and a full psychological profile.

"Early self-reliance due to orphan status, conscious rejection of authority due to deviation from proscribed worldviews, Anomalous beliefs and abilities, strongly-worded recommendation for neutralization. These are not qualities that we look for in our initiates. Luckily, we can design missions that don't require the conscious cooperation of the participants." With a few quick gestures, he pulled up another window with a different document, this one mostly text. "You're very devoted to your cause, Sarah. You're also a practical woman. When I put a million dollars in your bank account, you'll use it for the mission, regardless of the source. And now that you know I'm watching, you'll avoid any Anomalous activity that would jeopardize your mission. As long as you don't make any more Anomalous public spectacles that threaten to destabilize society, you're free to do whatever it takes to solve the problem."

Sarah's eyes widened. "A million dollars? No strings attached?"

"Yes. I've been looking for someone like you for over two years — a devoted climate activist with profound and as-yet-unquantified Anomalous qualities. Your defiant attitude is a vital part of the equation. You and your little band of friends over there may be the only wild card that can change the future."

"No pressure, right?"

The Preceptor laughed. "None at all."

Without a word, the Preceptor turned off the display on the wall and started walking, motioning for Sarah to follow. After a minute of walking, they found Patricia, Taliesin, and Hart standing in front of a scale model of Wardenclyffe Tower, the wireless telecommunication tower designed by Nikola Tesla. When Patricia saw the Preceptor approaching, her face twisted into an angry scowl.

"You!" She ran up to the Preceptor and stopped just short of him, pointing at him emphatically. "How could you do that to Tesla! You set electrical engineering back a century!"

The Preceptor smirked, holding his hands up in mock surrender. "Hey, don't look at me. I wasn't born yet. Order has started integrating his technologies. He was just a man ahead of his time."

Patricia crossed her arms, still glaring at the Preceptor. "You can't keep science on a leash forever!"

"I don't intend to. Not all science. Not forever." The Preceptor smiled warmly, opening his arms wide and turning slightly to face the entire group. "Congratulations! You're free to go. The elevator will take you up to the minimum security complex on the surface. Good luck!"

Without another word, the Preceptor turned away and started walking toward the exit.. Hart and Patricia both glared at him with crossed arms as he disappeared from sight. Taliesin looked off into the distance, lost in thought. Sarah laughed, shaking her head in disbelief.

"Really? That's it? Alright then."

Once the Preceptor was gone, Patricia's expression brightened. "Ooh! Can we stay a while longer and look at all the exhibits? It's so fascinating to see what they consider Anomalous and how it's changed over time. It may also reveal some valuable information about how to resist the Order. I wish I had my gear with me, but I have a photographic memory, so I—"

Hart raised a hand to interrupt Patricia. "We should go. It isn't safe here."

"If he were going to kill us, he would've done it by

now. Looking around for a few minutes should be fine. But let's be quick about it. Stick together and don't touch anything."

Patricia's eyes brightened. "Yay!"

For a few minutes, they walked together up and down the aisles of the museum. In the exhibits from the distant past, the biggest concern seemed to be inhuman creatures — faeries luring people to their deaths, trolls and shape-shifters killing people, demons summoned by strange blood rituals. Exhibits from the 19th century onward focused on more human concerns — humans displaying powerful supernatural abilities, cult leaders using various forms of mind control, strange devices that were destroyed or banned for the sake of public safety. There was even an exhibit on climate change that featured photos, graphs, and several climate projections that Sarah was very familiar with. It affirmed that human fossil fuel use was driving the climate crisis. The final paragraph described the situation as a classic example of what happens when formerly Anomalous technology is accepted into the global consensus without fully considering the consequences.

After looking over the exhibits, they walked to the exit together. As Taliesin, Patricia, and Hart, eagerly hurried down the hallway and filed into the elevator, Sarah lingered on the threshold for a moment, quietly reflecting on all that she had seen and heard. Eventually, she let the door close behind her and followed the others to the elevator. As promised, the elevator carried them up to the surface.

CHAPTER 11

*"Climate is changing.
Billions blind to the horror.
Tell a new story."*
— Bertram Muhnugin, The Death of Birth

The Student Ecology Center was bustling with new activity. The characteristic summer swelter of June in Southern Illinois was already in full swing. Half a dozen student interns were working in the garden, watering plants beneath the cloudless blue sky and laying down cardboard sheet mulch and fresh compost in the late morning heat and heavy humidity. Another outdoor team consisting of three young men and one woman was working on the parking lot, clearing away tall grass and thorny brambles to make room for two new parking spaces, a new bike rack, and an electric vehicle charging station. Inside the two-story air-conditioned geodesic dome at the south end of the property, three paid interns and a dozen volunteers were making phone calls and tapping away at laptop keyboards, slowly but surely making their way through a large national database of people who had expressed interest in supporting climate change activism.

Sarah and Hart pulled into the parking lot riding two similar electric motorcycles. They were the same make and model, but hers was a solid kelly green while his was mostly black with his characteristic hart logo emblazoned on the body. They parked side by side, waved to the outdoor workers, and walked down the path to enter the building.

"Sarah!"

The exclamation came from a woman sitting behind Sarah's desk. She was in her late twenties, short, round, olive-skinned, and wore a short sleeved blouse and slacks. Her deep brown eyes shone intensely from behind her thick glasses, and she sprang to her feet as she called out Sarah's name.

"Katie!" Sarah walked over to the woman and gave her a hug. "Has it been a busy morning?"

"Yes!" She picked up a stack of a half dozen small pieces of paper. "Bill McKibben called about partnering with 350.org. Someone from Grist Magazine wants to do an interview about the Green Goes Global project. Oh, and two more reporters called for interviews about the showdown with Percival Sword. One of them was from France."

Sarah grinned. As she had predicted, her trip to the IPC over a month ago had sparked an international debate about the role of the IPC and PEN News in spreading disinformation about climate change. Percival Sword was a very public figure, but never accepted unplanned interviews, so Sarah's appearance and subsequent arrest at the press conference had made big headlines on an otherwise slow news day. Patricia's Anomalous Revolution friends quickly ensured that the video and story went viral, leading millions of people to question what think tanks like IPC were saying about climate change and ask why a climate activist would be shot with tranquilizer darts for speaking at a press conference. Sarah had spoken to dozens of reporters about the "Showdown in St. Louis" over the course of the past month, including several from international news agencies. So far, she hadn't told anyone about their strange experiences at the Preceptory.

"Looks like I picked the wrong day to come in late!"

Hart walked up beside her and smiled, patting her lightly on the shoulder.

"It's always this busy. You needed a break."

Sarah laughed. "Yeah, yeah. I'm glad I have a superhero here to tell me when to take a break."

Hart's full superhero costume drew curious looks from two of the new volunteers. He wasn't wearing the mask, but the black body armor and heavy utility belt made him stand out on a hot summer day in a room full of T-shirts and shorts. Hart smiled and waved politely at the new volunteers, but they both looked back down at their computer screens without saying a word.

Sarah pulled up a chair next to Katie and started talking to her about the Green Goes Global project. Hart pulled out his tablet computer and cell phone and started calling phone numbers in the database.

For the rest of the day, they worked together at the Student Ecology Center. The volunteers ebbed and flowed, with some going to and from classes and most leaving early in the afternoon to carpool to an event across town. Hart left briefly to run errands, but soon returned to resume his calling duties.

At five in the afternoon, Taliesin walked in the front door.

"Taliesin!" Sarah jumped out of her chair and hurried over to Taliesin to give him a big bear hug. "How have you been?"

Taliesin returned the hug, holding Sarah for an extra moment before letting go and continuing.

"I've been well! Sorry I've been out of touch. Between wrapping up things at work, and the Coven, and trying to get Patricia out of that warehouse, I've been busy."

"How is Patricia?" Sarah's smile faded into a somber look. "Is she doing alright?"

"Oh, she's getting there." He paused, searching for words. "She was such a shut-in before we met her. She really wants to spend more time with us, but getting shot in the park didn't help. We've started taking trips outside with her little friend David, though. I think she'll be ready to come and visit soon."

"It's funny you should mention road trips. That's why I wanted to see you."

Sarah motioned for Hart to join them. Hart was one of the last volunteers left for the day. He was still on the phone with another caller. After a few moments, he said a warm goodbye to the caller and walked over to Sarah.

"Taliesin! Good to see you again."

"Good to see you too!"

The two men hugged each other, then both turned to Sarah expectantly. Sarah clasped her hands together in front of her chest and smiled broadly, a hint of mischief in her eyes.

"So, gentlemen. You're probably wondering why I've gathered you here today."

"Uh oh." Taliesin grinned. "This sounds serious."

"Yes, it's serious. Serious, but also exciting. You see, we're going on a road trip."

Taliesin's smile faded. Hart blinked, his brows furrowing in disbelief.

"We are?"

"Yes!" Sarah walked over to Hart's tablet computer and cell phone, picking them up and handing them to him. "We've set up a good activist campaign here: phone calls, letter writing, demonstrations, street theatre, legislative proposals. It's all wonderful, and it's a necessary baseline, but it's too traditional. It's not enough. We need something more, something unconventional, something magical, something that goes beyond traditional activist strategies and the analysis of the Preceptor. And I need to wander. So let's go."

She picked up her motorcycle helmet off of the desk and started walking toward the door. Hart grabbed his helmet, shaking his head with a sigh and following after Sarah. Taliesin paused in place for a moment, trying to voice an objection.

"But... I... where are we going?"

Sarah stopped near the door to reply. "First to St. Louis to pick up Patricia. Then the Midwest Renewable Energy Fair in Wisconsin. After that, who knows. How does that sound?"

Taliesin laughed. "Honestly? It sounds random. And impulsive. How long have you been planning this?"

"Longer than my last trip to St. Louis." Sarah smirked. "See you at Patricia's place!"

Sarah walked out the door. Hart shrugged, grinning sheepishly at Taliesin.

"Sorry, Tal. I would've warned you if I'd known."

"Oh, it's fine." Taliesin smiled. "She gets this way when she's inspired. You'd better catch her before she leaves, otherwise you'll be riding alone to St. Louis."

Hart nodded and hurried out the door. Taliesin looked around the room for a moment, waved goodbye to the handful of remaining volunteers, then headed out into the parking lot.

The Midwest Renewable Energy Fair was a massive gathering of over 20,000 people in the heart of rural central Wisconsin. The main area of the fair consisted of a small city's worth of canopy tents of various shapes and sizes standing in open fields beneath the blazing midsummer sun. The tents were home to every imaginable item related to renewable energy and green living: solar modules, wind turbines, solar hot water, geothermal air conditioning, alternative construction, ecological farming and gardening, and many different workshops and information booths about related topics. There was also music, food, massage, and various other amenities for the assembled crowd. Another area was dedicated to hundreds of personal tents of people choosing to camp rather than stay in a hotel. It was, in essence, a fully furnished tent city that appeared once a year in rural Wisconsin to promote renewable energy and ecological living.

Sarah, Hart, Patricia, and Taliesin wandered up and down the aisles of the fair, browsing various exhibits and splitting up every now and then to cover more ground. Patricia was endlessly fascinated by the technical displays, darting back and forth to talk to each vendor for a few minutes about technical details of manufacturing and performance that a salesperson or installer may or may not be aware of. Hart browsed the tents with polite half-interest, occasionally drawn in by information about back-to-the-land survivalist techniques and equipment. Sarah and Taliesin wandered idly together, talking to a few of the vendors and stopping for a while to listen to music.

It was Taliesin who noticed a somewhat familiar face at one of the solar energy booths.

"Hey, isn't he from Southern Illinois?"

Sarah followed Taliesin's gaze.

"Aur!"

Aur Beck was a stocky man in his late thirties with long brown hair in a ponytail, tan skin, and close-trimmed beard ending in a longer goatee. He was wearing sunglasses with mirror lenses, khaki pants, and a crisp blue button-up shirt with a company logo where the left pocket would otherwise be. His booth at the fair consisted of a white canopy tent, a trailer with a colorful red and orange logo that said "Advanced Energy Solutions", and a table with a display about solar energy, including a few small toys and a full-sized solar module.

"Hey!"

Aur saw Sarah approaching and opened his arms wide. They hugged for a long moment before Aur continued.

"How are you? I thought you couldn't make it this year because of that new project. What's it called, Green Goes Global?"

"My friend Katie's taking care of the details. I can only go to so many meetings before I start to go crazy. I needed to wander again."

Aur chuckled. "I know what you mean."

Taliesin walked up and waved to Aur.

"Hello. Aur is it?"

"Yes it is. Aur 'Da Energy Mon' at your service."

The two men shook hands.

"I'm Sarah's friend Taliesin."

"Ah, Taliesin. I couldn't remember, but I knew it was something interesting. So how do you like the Fair?"

"It's great." Taliesin looked around at all of the

surrounding tents and the endless stream of people moving among them. "I've always meant to learn more about green living, but hanging out with Sarah has really opened my eyes. And this place is a showcase of everything I've been learning."

"Exactly." Aur smiled. "I come here once a year to remind myself why I do what I do. All these people come here, and each one of them is working on a different solution for sustainable living. I do solar installation, somebody else does geothermal, somebody else does green building. Put it all together and you get a green society." He shrugged. "Or at least as close as we can get, right?"

Taliesin nodded. "Right."

Sarah felt a sudden flash of inspiration. Before she even knew what she was saying, she started speaking.

"Aur, this activist campaign is a start, but it isn't enough. We came here looking for something different, something more, something that nobody will see coming. Something that will inspire the change in consciousness that people here are looking for. What would you recommend?"

"Hmm." Aur leaned back a bit, stroking his goatee thoughtfully. "Well you need to start with the activist campaign. I read an article about your idea to start little green think tanks in every community. That's good. Every community needs to come up with its own ideas."

He looked off into the distance, searching for something. After a few moments, his eyes brightened and he snapped his fingers as the idea came to him.

"You should work on the culture. People don't always listen to rational explanations. They'll listen, but first you have to give them a reason to. You have to tell a story — a story that they want to listen to. It could be a song, or a book, or a movie. People think it's too hard to go green, or they get depressed about how big and bad climate change is, so they give up. You should find people who can make them laugh and cry and feel a part of something bigger. Then every day will be like a green fair, and everyone will get involved in their own way."

As Aur spoke, Sarah slipped into a mild trance, her mind racing with visions of writers, artists, and musicians working alone and together on projects related to to climate change, renewable energy, and ecological living. The visions culminated in the image of a lone man with a translucent guitar standing on stage in front of a massive audience at a stadium that was packed to capacity. Somehow, Sarah knew that his voice was the keynote that would inspire millions of new people to take action on her climate change initiatives.

Sarah snapped out of her trance and laughed.

"Exactly!" She gave Aur a big hug. "That gives me so many ideas. More than ideas — visions. I hate to do this to you, but I need to go."

Aur chuckled. "Oh, I see how it goes. Take my good ideas and leave?"

"Yes." She reached into her pocket and handed him a business card. "Call my friend Katie though and tell her you're the solar installer I mentioned. We need some solar at the Student Ecology Center."

Aur took the card and nodded with a smile. "Will do."

"Alright, I'll see you around!"

Sarah bounded off in search of Hart and Patricia. Taliesin waved to Aur.

"Good to see you!"

Aur chuckled. "You too. Stay energized!"

CHAPTER 12

*"Peacock, green and blue
The eyes of the world on you.
Will you sing for change?"*
— Bertram Muhnugin, The Death of Birth

Soldier Field was filled to capacity with the crowd for the night's sold out concert. Over 65,000 people of all ages, colors, shapes, and sizes were packed into the seats on the field, in the stands, and in the sky boxes of the stadium. Thousands more were gathered in the July heat of the streets and parks of the surrounding area just to be close to to the main event: the music and stage presence of emerging rock legend Jonny Glas.

Sarah had managed to secure four tickets just a few rows away from the main stage. Hart, however, had decided to join his superhero colleagues out in the streets of Chicago to help manage the chaos of the enormous crowd. As the concert was about to start, Sarah, Taliesin, and Patricia found their seats near the stage. Patricia placed her robotic gnome David in the seat next to hers, tucking her bag beneath him so that he would have a better view of the show.

Sarah turned around and looked out at the sprawling crowd. Usually, her default expression was fairly neutral, bordering on stern. Tonight, she was warm and glowing, soaking up the boisterous energy of the crowd at what was by far the biggest concert that she had ever attended.

Taliesin turned to Patricia. "Are you doing alright?"

"Yes!" Patricia was even more wide-eyed and fidgety than usual, in spite of the fact that they had avoided caffeine all night. "So much to see and it hasn't even started yet! I've never been to a concert before. Is it okay if I dance? I always dance when I'm listening to Jonny Glas at home but do they do that at concerts? They do sometimes in the videos, but sometimes they don't."

Taliesin smiled. "Yes, go ahead and dance, even if nobody else is." He gave Patricia a big hug and quick kiss. "Remember what we talked about at the hotel though, okay?"

"What we talked about? Oh yeah, that." A mischievous grin flashed across her face. "No hacking the jumbotron. Not even a little. It's a slippery slope."

"Yes, exactly."

As they settled into their seats, the lights dimmed and the show began.

The lights and displays on stage were all off or dim, leaving the stadium in relative darkness. The bustle and chatter of the audience faded into a quiet stillness as the darkness lingered for over a minute. Suddenly, a spotlight illuminated a lone figure on the long walkway leading up to the stage.

Jonny Glas stood at the threshold of the walkway with his guitar held high overhead. As soon as he was visible, the audience went wild, clapping and whooping and crying his name. His brilliant blue-green eyes shined with a fierce intensity as he spun slowly in place to present himself and his instrument to the entire stadium. He had a wispy, almost ethereal look, with elegantly gaunt features, short spiked hair, loose-fitting silk shirt and silk bell bottoms, and pointy shoes. His clothes, guitar, long eyelashes, eyeshadow, and blush were all various blended shades of blue and green that shifted and shimmered as he moved. His skin was pale, almost ashen in contrast to the bold peacock colors of his outfit.

Once he had finished turning in place, Jonny slung his guitar over his shoulder with a cocky grin and strutted toward the stage. The lights blinked to life as he walked by, illuminating the stadium bit by bit until he reached the stage and the entire crowd was suddenly bathed in electric luminescence. The layout of the stage was simple, with several large screens behind him and a jumbotron overhead to display the performance for people sitting in the most distant seats. The screens and arch were framed in elaborate blue and green Celtic knotwork interwoven with wreaths of fresh oak and holly.

When Jonny reached the center of the stage, just below the central arch, he swung his guitar in front of him and placed his left hand on the neck of the instrument, holding his right hand just slightly away from the strings, as though he were about to strum. The roar of the crowd rose to a wild crescendo, and he paused for a long moment, basking in the boisterous energy of the tens of thousands of people cheering and chanting his name. Finally, he strummed the strings and started to play.

The entire concert was a one-man performance. He started with one of his earliest songs, a lively folk ballad about life on the road. With the push of a button, he changed the tone of his instrument from acoustic guitar to fiddle and played a lively Irish jig, dancing to the music without skipping a beat. For the next song, he switched to electric guitar and played some hard rock, alternately strutting across the stage and rocking in place as he sang about seeing life as an endless party. Then, he switched back to an acoustic sound, and the crowd thundered with applause as they recognized the opening chords to his most popular song of all.

As he started the song, he casually scanned the audience with a broad smile. Suddenly, his eyes met Sarah's, and both of their hearts skipped a beat. She wasn't in the front row, but she was close enough to the stage that he could actually look into her eyes. He was still smiling, and there was still a warmth to his expression, but the confidence had been replaced by a tender vulnerability. He eventually broke the gaze and continued with the song, but looked back at her every time he reached the refrain.

> "But there you were
> As plain as day
> And the moment I saw you
> I knew just what to say
> And the moment I saw you
> I knew just what to do
> I will always wander, love
> but I thank the stars above
> that from this day onward, love
> I will wander with you"

Sarah's heart quickened and eyes widened as Jonny sang to her. Most of the audience couldn't tell who exactly he was singing to or didn't even notice at all that his eyes kept returning to the same person. But everyone near Sarah, including Taliesin and Patricia, looked back and forth between Jonny and Sarah in amazement. Jonny finished the song, and as the crowd burst into thunderous applause, he pointed at Sarah with a sly smile.

"You there with the beautiful green eyes! See me after the show!"

Sarah laughed, her face flushed with amusement and excitement. Taliesin and Patricia stared at her in disbelief. Before they could say anything, Jonny started the next song, and the show continued.

Throughout the rest of the show, Jonny would glance back at Sarah occasionally. His music continued flowing from genre to genre, focusing mostly on rock, folk, and trance music. The small buttons on his guitar allowed him to emulate various instruments such as a fiddle, a flute, a piano, bells, a theremin, and several distinct synthetic tones which he looped during his trance music. The screens on stage mostly showed him playing, but sometimes interspersed rustic outdoor scenes during the folk music and abstract patterns of swirling colors and lights during the rock and trance. Finally, he concluded with a high energy rock song about the power of music to change the world, with most of the audience singing along. As he spoke his last words and strummed his last chord, the crowd cheered and applauded. They continued cheering as he took a deep bow, left the stage, walked down the walkway, and showed off his instrument one last time before disappearing from sight.

Sarah stood in the elevator lobby of the Hard Rock Hotel Chicago, idly examining the polished marble walls and intricate engravings adorning the brass elevator doors. A handful of people were waiting on one of the other elevators, dressed in knockoff designer clothes and chatting casually about celebrities who they may or may not have actually met. Their elevator arrived first, so Sarah was briefly alone in the lobby, listening to the murmur of distant voices and the hum of machinery echoing in the elevator shafts. Finally, the elevator door opened, revealing the man in a peacock blue suit who had brought Sarah to the hotel.

"He's ready to see you now."

Sarah stepped into the elevator. As the doors slid shut behind her, the man in blue pressed a button and the elevator slid into motion.

"Does he invite a lot of fans to meet him after the show?"

The otherwise quiet man laughed suddenly.

"Lady, he doesn't even talk to his staff after shows. He says he's too busy 'integrating the magic of the music'." The man shrugged with a chuckle, then looked her up and down with a broadening smile. "I don't know exactly what it is about you, but I see it too. You have a certain glow about you. How he spotted it from twenty yards away in the middle of a concert, I'll never know. The man has a gift."

The elevator doors opened, and the man silently gestured for her to step forward. She nodded, stepping out of the elevator and walking up to the door at the end of the hallway.

Sarah's pulse quickened as she knocked on the door and awaited a response. After a few moments, she heard footsteps, and the door slid open.

Jonny's outfit and appearance was even more remarkable up close than it had been at a distance. His eyes were a distinctive blue-green-grey blend that varied in color based on lighting and mood. His hair and clothes were iridescent, blending shades of blue and green that shifted and shimmered as he moved. His guitar was still slung over his shoulder with the strap across his chest and the neck visible behind his head. His ashen skin was soft and smooth, and his lips were thin but lively, spreading into a broad smile as his eyes glimmered with recognition.

"It's a pleasure to see you again." He extended his hand in greeting. "My name's Jonny."

Sarah laughed, shaking his hand with a grin. "Yes, I know your name. My name's Sarah."

"Of course. Please, do come in."

The suite was far more elegant than any hotel room Sarah had ever stayed in, but not as wildly extravagant as she had imagined the hotel room of a rock star. It featured a dining area and living room furnished with a sleek grey leather couch and seats, large windows covered with grey curtains, a slim green vase holding a single blue rose, and a large flat screen TV.

"Please, feel free to have a seat. Would you like anything to drink?"

Sarah sat down on the couch and glanced over at the dining area.

"Is that red wine?"

"Yes, it is."

"May I have some of that?"

"Yes, you may."

Jonny uncorked the bottle and poured two full glasses of wine, handing one to Sarah and sitting in the chair closest to her spot on the couch. They clinked their glasses together and each took a long drink.

"I really enjoyed the concert tonight."

"Then it was all worth it."

Sarah smiled. "What was it about me that caught your eye in a sea of thousands of faces? How did you even see me out there in the crowd?"

"How could anyone not see you?" As Jonny looked at Sarah, his eyes brightened, and his face bloomed into an expression of childlike wonder. "Everyone has a certain energy to them. Yours is unlike any I've ever seen. You stand with the quiet strength of a mountain. You flow like the river finding its way to the ocean. Your heart burns with an unquenchable flame that carries you through the darkness. I don't know what you've come here looking for, but I know you're looking for something. And I know I've been looking for you for a long time."

Sarah's eyes widened and pulse quickened. She took several long gulps of wine and let the words sink in for a few moments before responding.

"Yes, I've come here looking for someone to help me inspire some important changes in the world." She grinned. "And I may have come to the right place."

"Here's hoping."

The two clinked their wine glasses together again and took another drink. Jonny set his glass aside, taking his guitar in hand and strumming the strings slowly. It was a mournful tune, and Jonny's face took on a mournful expression as he played it.

"Discord. Cacophony. Imbalance."

The tempo started out very slow, but increased slightly with each measure. Jonny closed his eyes, listening intently to the music. After a while, he started speaking in rhythm with the music:

> *"Human invention it sets the intention*
> *to change the world, change the world.*
> *Spiraling motion and sudden commotion*
> *estrange the world, strange the world.*
> *Building and growing and learning and knowing*
> *the pages turn, pages turn.*
> *Killing and maiming and screaming and blaming,*
> *the sages burn, sages burn."*

Jonny kept strumming faster and faster, his face twisting in an agonizing grimace. Finally, he slammed his strumming hand on the strings to silence them. For a moment, he sat there in silence, his eyes closed and his face heavy with a lingering look of pain. Finally, he took a deep breath, let out a long sigh, and opened his eyes to look at Sarah.

"You're a braver soul than I am, love." He smiled wistfully, looking off into the distance as he continued. "I find myself lost in a breathless mix of wonder and terror as I wander the winding road of a single human heart. You find yourself surrounded by countless voices crying out at the destruction of an entire world — and instead of running away, you delve deeper, searching for the source of their sorrow."

Sarah found herself at a loss for words. She didn't tend to think of herself in such dramatic terms, but she couldn't disagree with his words either.

"I do what I can."

Jonny laughed, a soulful sound that echoed through the empty hotel room and resonated deeply with Sarah.

"That's just it, Sarah. You do what you can't."

Jonny picked up his guitar again, strumming slowly and listening to the music.

"You do what you can't. Therein lies the magic. There is no way that one person can stand against the madness of a million fools and the sadness of the seven billion who follow them. The music foretells a climate apocalypse in our future, and I see no way to change that tune. But change it you will, and change it we will. And as we will it, so mote it be."

The melody took a more lively, almost hypnotic turn, and Sarah felt her pulse quicken with the tempo. For a moment, she was reminded of her vision in the church — pulsing channels of causality stretching out in every direction, connecting her to the people and places around her. As Jonny played, she could feel the channels vibrating and hear them humming like strings on a guitar. Strum the strings in the right order and the notes become cords, synchronous changes in people and places that would seem like magic to someone who couldn't hear or feel the music.

For a long time, they listened to the music together. Eventually, Jonny's playing drifted into silence. After sitting with her in the silence for a while, he eventually spoke.

"My head tells me that I can't do what you're asking. I can't possibly use the power of music to persuade millions of people to do something more daring than buying my next album. But you inspire me, Sarah. You inspire me to do what I believe I can't possibly do."

Jonny's eyes ignited with a sudden intensity. He gulped down the last of his wine and leapt to his feet, tossing the glass aside.

"What a breath of fresh air! I can feel the fire of change flowing through my veins! My flesh is alive with new purpose!"

He strummed a few frantic cords on his guitar, taking a step toward Sarah and leaning toward her slightly with a sly smile.

"I have six more stops on this tour. If you'll come away with me, I'll sing the songs of change along the way. What do you say?"

Sarah rose to her feet. She finished her wine, setting the glass aside and taking a step toward Jonny.

"If my friends can join us for the journey, we've got a deal."

"Your friends are my friends, and your journey my journey." He slid his guitar onto his back, stepping in closer and placing his hand on the small of her back. "As long as we travel together, the journey will be a good one."

As they looked into each others eyes, their lips met, joining in a long and lingering kiss. They wrapped their arms around each other and kissed again, holding each other close and losing themselves in the sound of the music.

CHAPTER 13

*"For change to be known
a woman of the people
must speak to the world."*
— Bertram Muhnugin, The Death of Birth

Several dozen people, most of them dressed in a variety of bold and colorful costumes, walked together in a cluster down West Franklin Boulevard in Chicago. Sarah, Taliesin, Patricia, Hart, and Jonny were at the head of the crowd, carrying bags of supplies and talking to the four reporters and two-person documentary crew that were trailing the group. After taking a few group shots, the reporters were most interested in talking to Hart and Jonny.

"We're meeting here today to drop off some donations we've collected for Interfaith House, a service center for ill and injured homeless adults. I myself received care and housing here several years ago, so I like to give back to the place that changed my life. Once we drop off the blankets and books and personal hygiene products in these donation bags, we'll be splitting into several groups to do homeless outreach in several different areas."

The reporter that was talking to Hart turned to Jonny, and several cameras were pointed his way.

"Jonny, what brought you out here on a Saturday morning?"

"Musicians are storytellers." He patted Hart on the back with his free hand. "This man's story inspires me. I've made a lot of money singing about love and heartache and whatnot. It's times to ease a few weary hearts by showing some basic human kindness."

"Does this mean you're becoming an activist?"

Jonny smiled. "I'm not one for labels, friend. I'm a creature of flesh and blood, not some byte of data in your news feed. What I will say is that I follow my heart, and my heart says it's time for a change."

Everyone in the crowd made several trips back and forth between the moving van full of supplies and the community center, dropping off bags and boxes of supplies that had been collected in the weeks leading up to the morning's delivery. Once the vehicles were empty, they split up into several groups and went their separate ways. Sarah and her companions went with Hart's old friends Pythia and Black and Blue to volunteer at a nearby homeless shelter and neighborhood resource center. After several hours of volunteering at the center and making a few food deliveries to local households, Sarah and her companions walked to a nearby park to relax and have a late lunch.

Garfield Park was a large green space on the west side of Chicago that featured numerous winding trails among the trees and grass, several sports fields and buildings, a large lagoon for fishing, and a conservatory. Sarah, Hart, and Jonny sat together in the August heat on an aging wood and concrete park bench looking out over the lagoon. Patricia and Taliesin wandered around nearby, using Patricia's tablet computer to search for a geocache hidden somewhere among the trees.

"I've got good news and bad news, love. Good news being that they said I can change the theme of the next five concerts however I like. Bad news being that I can't change the dates or locations. Seems that once you sell hundreds of thousands of concert tickets, they're not fond of changing the dates."

Sarah laughed. "That's fair. Your next concert's in a week though, right? Will that give you enough time to make all the changes?"

Jonny smirked, pulling out his guitar and playing a few cords. "I could write an album in less if the mood were right. And it is, it is." He closed his eyes for a moment, listening to the sound of the music as he played. "I need to do some reading. Maybe watch a documentary or two about the climate crisis. And I need you to tell me what inspired you to get into this work. I know a fair bit about the facts, but it's not about the facts, it's about the feel of it. What does it feel like to watch the world burn? And what does it feel like to take a stand?"

Jonny strummed his guitar, keeping his eyes closed and holding his ear closer to the strings. For a few moments, they sat together without speaking, listening to the music.

Suddenly, Sarah felt a sinking feeling in the pit of her stomach. Jonny's music slowed to a stop and Hart rose to his feet, his eyes drawn to a dot in the sky. The unmarked black helicopter approached almost impossibly quickly and quietly, transforming from a small black dot in the distance to a large aircraft hovering overhead. The helicopter touched down almost silently in the grass a few yards away from the park bench, and Hart stood protectively in front of Sarah and Jonny, motioning to Taliesin and Patricia to stay back.

As the helicopter's blades started slowing to a stop, a door on the side of the craft slid open. A handsome young man in an elegant white tuxedo with a black bow tie and white gloves took a single step onto the ground and stood at attention, one hand extended in a gesture of welcoming.

"Miss Athraigh, I presume?"

Sarah brushed aside Hart's protective hands and took a step forward, peering deeply into the man's eyes with stern expression.

"Who's asking?"

"Miss Athraigh, I have been sent by Doctor Truman Stuart, Preceptor of Order, to invite you and four guests to an exclusive celebration being held tonight for the benefit of the Foundation for the Advancement of the Initiation of a Transcendent Humanity."

Sarah smirked. "You've come to invite me to a party?"

"Yes, ma'am. The Preceptor sends his apologizes for the belated arrival and unusual nature of the invitation. You were not at your place of your residence and not available by phone."

"Is this invitation voluntary?"

"Yes, ma'am. Should you choose to accept, we will transport you to the event and return you to the destination of your choice whenever you choose to depart."

"Alright. Give me a minute here."

Sarah turned to Hart and Jonny. Taliesin and Patricia cautiously approached, with Taliesin casting a wary glance at the helicopter while Patricia stuck her tongue out at the attendant.

Sarah lowered her voice to a near whisper. "So what do you think? I'd like to see what he's up to."

"I'm always in the mood for a good party." Jonny smiled broadly, a glimmer of mischief in his eyes. "If that's our ride, I can only imagine what the rest of the party looks like."

Taliesin shrugged. "I don't like it, but I suppose there's no harm in it. If he wanted to kill us, he would've done it already."

As Patricia tapped on her tablet computer for a few moments, her scornful expression suddenly shifted into a look of childlike glee. "Ooh, ooh! It must be the super secret annual party at Providence Catalysis! We have to go!"

Hart crossed his arm, his otherwise gentle face clenched with anger. "Must I always be the voice of reason? This is a man who kidnapped us. This is a man who uses his money and power to corrupt governments and control the course of world events. He is not to be trusted."

"I never said that I trust him." Sarah smiled sweetly, patting Hart on the shoulder affectionately. "I just said we should go."

Hart sighed, shaking his head. "I will go with you wherever your journey takes you. But you're playing with fire."

"No, he's the one playing with fire." Sarah's expression grew more serious as she looked off into the distance. "I am the fire of change, the flickering flame that burns slow but steady through the long nights of Winter, waiting for the moment to flash into the light of Spring."

Sarah turned to face the attendant, placing a comforting hand on Hart's back as she spoke.

"I accept your invitation."

"Excellent, Miss Athraigh. Please, come this way."

The attendant made a welcoming gesture toward the interior of the helicopter, inviting them to board. Sarah took Hart by the hand and stepped forward, followed by Jonny, Patricia, and Taliesin. The inside of the craft was like a limousine, complete with plush leather seating, a television, and a bottle of champaign chilling on ice with five champaign glasses. As they took their seats, the attendant stepped on board and closed the door behind them. The helicopter sprang to life and took to the air, whisking them away just as quickly and quietly as it had landed.

Providence Catalysis was a colonial-era mansion standing alone in a circular clearing on a peak in the Appalachian Mountains. The red brick building consisted of a large two-story central block with connecting hallways leading to two additional wings with slightly rounded facades that were each half as large as the main structure. The building had numerous mirrored windows, a white roof and columns, a meticulously trimmed topiary garden featuring numerous elaborate abstract shapes, and four life-sized marble angel statues. The angels were kneeling on either side of the cobblestone path leading up to the front door, their hands clasped in prayer and their heads bowed in deference to those who passed between them.

Sarah and her companions walked the short distance from the cobblestone helipad to the front door. They had been asked not to bring any cameras, but Patricia used her tablet computer to take a few quick photos of the building and statues. Hart eyed the building warily, squinting at the mirrored windows in a vain effort to see inside. Jonny pulled out his guitar and pressed the small buttons on the edge to adjust the tone, strumming the strings to create the sound of a harp as they walked between the angels. Just before they reached the doorstep, the door swung open, and another attendant dressed in a white tuxedo welcomed them inside.

The interior was more spacious than Sarah had imagined. The teal walls were framed in white wood trim and adorned with over a dozen life-size portrait paintings of mostly men in clothing ranging from colonial era to the present day. The entryway opened up into a large dining room and two slightly smaller lounges, all three of which were filled nearly to capacity with people standing in small groups or sitting around tables talking to each other over drinks and hors d'œuvre. Glancing among the well-dressed attendees, Sarah quickly recognized several famous people, including a former vice-president, the CEO of a major energy corporation, a notoriously wealthy movie star, and a former prime minister of England.

"Sarah Athraigh!"

Sarah and her companions turned to see the smiling face of the Preceptor approaching them. He was dressed in a black evening tailcoat, white shirt and bow tie, a low-cut white waistcoat, and a golden sash with a bold embroidered black "O" with a white center.

"Glad you could make it!" The Preceptor shook everyone's hand, starting with Sarah and finishing with Jonny. "You must be Jonny Glas! It's a pleasure to have a genuine rock star among us."

"Quite a fancy shindig you've got here." Jonny lifted a glass of wine from a passing server's tray and took a quick drink. "You're the one with the fancy secret base, then, and the golden crown and such?"

The Preceptor smiled warmly, lifting a finger to his lips

to shush Jonny playfully.

"Our little secret. Come, let me introduce you to a few of the other guests."

The Preceptor led the group into the dining room, introducing each of Sarah's companions to a different person. He introduced Taliesin to the founder of a spiritual healing school, Patricia to a scientist who was involved in a particle accelerator research program, Hart to the director of an academic non-profit that was studying Real Life Superheroes, and Jonny to one of his biggest fans who also happened to be a billionaire.

As her companions split off to focus on side conversations, Sarah walked with the Preceptor toward the stairs to the second floor. Before they started up the steps, however, Sarah saw a familiar face out of the corner of her eye.

"Percy!"

Before the Preceptor could object, Sarah strode confidently toward Percival Sword, owner of the PSI Entertainment Network and its flagship media outlet, PEN News. Percival stood at the center of one of the side lounges, dressed in a black silk blazer and surrounded by a dozen women and half a dozen men as he smiled broadly and told charming stories with a twinkle in his eye and smooth, sweeping gestures to punctuate key points.

"And I said, 'If being successful is wrong, I don't want to be right!'"

Everyone in the room laughed, even a few people who appeared to be involved in side conversations. Before he could continue with his next story, however, Sarah made her way through the crowd and repeated his name.

"Percy! The infamous Percival Sword! Fancy meeting you here."

Percival smiled warmly at Sarah, casting a cold glance over her shoulder at the Preceptor before returning his attention to her.

"Why, if it isn't Little Miss Chicken Little! Have you had a chance to check out that news site I recommended?"

Everyone in the circle around Percival chuckled. Sarah

smirked, brushing away the Preceptor's restraining hand before continuing.

"Yes, actually. And don't worry, I'll let you return to your little fan club in a minute here. I just have one question."

"Oh?" Percival smiled with genuine curiosity. As he looked into Sarah's eyes, his icy blue pupils contracted slightly, and she felt as if he were peering into the depths of her soul. "This should be entertaining. And I am ever the entertainer, so do tell."

Sarah glared at his warm smile and calculating eyes.

"We both know the truth about climate change, but you don't seem to know what's coming. Will all of your money and power protect you when climate disasters create social upheaval that tears apart the very fabric of reality as we know it?"

For a long moment, Percival stared at her in silence, the smile fading from his lips. Then, he clapped his hands together in front of his chest, smiling broadly and extending his clasped hands in her direction.

"Bravo, Chicken Little! You're the only one here who gives a more dramatic speech than I do. Bravo!"

Percival started clapping, and everyone around him followed suit. Just as Sarah was about to reply, she heard the Preceptor's voice whispering in her ear.

"Not now."

The Preceptor started walking back toward the stairs and motioned for Sarah to follow. Sarah looked back at Percival for a moment, pointing a finger at him with an angry glare.

"This isn't over, Sword. Change is coming, and you're in the way."

She brushed aside the Preceptor and pushed through the crowd, marching out of the room and back to the foot of the stairs. After a few moments, the Preceptor caught up to her, leaning in close to speak to her in hushed tones.

"You're the life of the party."

"What can I say. I have a conscience."

"That you do."

Sarah sighed in exasperation. "You say you want to do something about climate change. Isn't dealing with people like him a good start? Can't you just—"

"Tread carefully, Sarah." He glanced in Percival's direction. "Direct confrontation is not the answer here. PEN News is one of the most advanced social engineering tools on the planet. He has more power than you can imagine. Fighting him head-on will get you nowhere."

"How else can I fight him? PEN is one of the worst climate science deniers on the planet. They're single-handedly brainwashing millions of people into believing that climate change isn't even happening. Doesn't that have to change in order to prevent the world from burning all the fossil fuels and triggering a climate apocalypse? Somebody has to stop them."

"You're still thinking like a rabble-rousing peasant, Sarah. Stop fighting the power and start being the power. Find your power and wield it like a queen. If you don't like the way that PEN is leading the people, lead them another way."

"Lead them another way? Like you do?" She crossed her arms and glared at the Preceptor. "I don't want to be a social engineer like you. I want to be an activist. I want to inspire people to make up their own minds and take their own actions to create a better world."

The Preceptor smiled broadly. "That, my dear, is the highest form of social engineering. Like the architect who captures the rays of the sun to heat and light a home, or the—"

An unfamiliar old man in an expensive suit suddenly walked up to the Preceptor, standing a little too close to him and ignoring Sarah.

"Truman!" The man's thin-lipped smile, slightly flushed face, and cold grey eyes spoke of a deep anger beneath the thin facade of polite greeting. "The rumors are true, then. You really are consorting with terrorists."

The Preceptor cringed, his head twisting and lips curling as he drew breath with an audible hiss.

"Miss Athraigh, this is Edward Richard Jamison, President of the Board of the International Prometheus

Consortium. Mr. Jamison, this is—"

"I know damned well who this is, Truman. I also know that one of your little front groups deposited a large sum of money in her bank account just days after she disrupted a press conference in front of our world headquarters."

"Miss Athraigh is an outside consultant. Her methods are unconventional, but—"

Jamison interrupted the Preceptor by placing a firm hand on his shoulder. "Come now, Truman. Have you been spending so much time in that little hideaway of yours that you've forgotten how things work out here in the real world? I speak on behalf of several members of the board who are very concerned about public perception of the petroleum industry. If these gentlemen knew exactly the sort of company you keep, they might not be so eager to fund your little social engineering operation."

The Preceptor nonchalantly drew a handgun out of a hidden holster and planted the cold steel muzzle in the middle of Jamison's forehead.

Jamison gasped, his eyes widening and jaw dropping. A hush fell over the entire room. The Preceptor stared at Jamison with a look of cold contempt, letting the silence linger for a long moment before speaking to Jamison in a calm but firm tone.

"You, sir, have forgotten how the real world works. I could end you right now and control your assets within two hours. You're a valuable asset, but like all assets, you are replaceable. Never forget that."

Jamison took several slow steps back, bowing slightly in deference to the Preceptor. The Preceptor slid his gun back into its holster, smiling broadly and sweeping his arms wide open in a welcoming gesture to the everyone in the room.

"So glad you could all make it! Please, have another drink on the house!"

The Preceptor grabbed a half-full glass of wine and casually headed toward the stairs. After exchanging confused looks and shrugged shoulders, the guests gradually returned to their various conversations. Sarah noticed that the Preceptor was already halfway up the steps and decided to follow him.

"Do you always brandish weapons at your party guests?"

The Preceptor smiled broadly. "Only the rude ones."

The upstairs was more closed off than the downstairs, with a long hallway leading to several side rooms in either direction. The Preceptor walked up to the second room on the right and invited her to step inside.

The room was relatively small, with enough space for a simple wooden office desk and an ornate wooden table with eight matching chairs. Two of the seats were empty, and Sarah didn't recognize five of the people at the table, all of whom hurried out of the room as soon as she and the Preceptor entered. The sixth person, however, was very familiar.

Irene O'Neill was a woman in her mid to late thirties with brown hair, brown eyes, a slightly round face, and a full figure. Her features were smooth and youthful, but her expression was serious, and her eyes shone with a warm intelligence that studied the people around her with a judicious balance of human warmth and careful calculation. She was wearing a charcoal grey suit jacket and slacks with a white blouse and hair up in a pony tail.

Sarah had never met Irene before, but she recognized her from the dozens of news articles she had read about her. She was a former community organizer who had just starting serving her first term of office in the U.S. House of Representatives.

"Sarah, allow me to introduce you to another new friend of mine. Sarah Athraigh, this is Congresswoman Irene O'Neill. Congresswoman O'Neill, this is Sarah Athraigh."

Sarah smiled broadly. "It's a pleasure to meet you, Congresswoman O'Neill."

"Please, call me Irene." She stood and approached Sarah, shaking her hand with a firm grip. "It's a pleasure to meet you as well. Not many people have had the pleasure of telling off Percival Sword in front of his own news cameras!"

Sarah and Irene laughed. The Preceptor chuckled, wagging his finger at Sarah with a sly smile.

"Naughty, naughty."

Sarah smirked. "I would have kept going if someone hadn't shot me full of tranquilizers."

The Preceptor laughed. "Yes, you would have. Discretion is the better part of valor, Sarah. Remember that next time."

"And the best defense is a good offense."

"I like your attitude, Sarah." Irene smiled warmly. "I can see what he sees in you. You remind me of myself before I became a politician. Bright, assertive, uncompromising."

"I've always been a big fan of yours. I would've voted for you if you were in my state."

"Thank you."

"Great!" The Preceptor clasped his hands together with a broad smile. "As you may know, Irene here has mostly focused on peace and social justice issues. She does, however, have some climate change news that may interest you. I'll let you two get to it!"

Without another word, the Preceptor slipped out the door, closing it behind himself to leave Sarah and Irene alone together.

Sarah looked at the door in mild disbelief, a slight smile on her lips. "He's so strange sometimes."

Irene chuckled. "Yes, he is." She paused, her expression becoming more somber. "Does he really have an underground base and a private army?"

"Oh, yes." Sarah looked at Irene quizzically. "You mean you haven't seen it? I was assuming the government was in on it."

"Government?" Irene sighed wistfully. "I wish I knew what that word meant anymore. I came into office full of hope and expectations. Now I know that it's all just a game — and the game is controlled by a handful of men with more money and power than all the world's governments put together. I doubt even the President has seen whatever it is that you've seen. I've only heard about it in whispers spoken on the condition of anonymity."

"Oh, it's pretty crazy." Sarah laughed. "He's got this big control room where he monitors the entire world for Anomalies, and this museum full of exhibits about how dangerous these Anomalies are, and a bunch of fancy gear that makes my techie friend Patricia drool."

Irene shook her head slowly. "I wonder if that's where some of the secret defense budget is going. The federal government spends tens of billions of dollars a year on 'black budget' projects that even most members of Congress aren't allowed to review. If there really are people out there with these dramatic abilities, though, I suppose we have to do something."

Sarah smirked. "Congressional review would be nice. I'll bet you wouldn't vote to put me and my friends in body bags."

Irene's eyes widened for a moment, then she smiled warmly, patting Sarah on the shoulder.

"No, Sarah, I definitely wouldn't."

"Thanks. On the bright side, he seems really concerned about climate change."

"Oh, yes." She picked up a hefty binder from the desk, paging through a lengthy report. "He's considered dozens of options, some of which are quite frankly horrific. It takes a disturbed mind to calmly describe the rapid elimination of 95% of the population." She shuddered, setting the binder back on the desk and pushing it away. "He concludes by arguing that the most promising and palatable solution is a program of targeted support for a handful of Anomalous individuals and organizations that may be capable of creating a rapid shift in global consciousness in an extremely short period of time."

Sarah grinned. "That would be me."

Irene smiled. "Yes, you first and foremost, though there are other plans, and plans within plans, and presumably even more plans that he's not telling either of us about."

"So what do we do?"

"If it's alright with you, Sarah, I'd like to spend a couple of weeks studying your approach and offering my assistance where possible. I've recently been appointed to the Joint Select Committee on Climate Change Mitigation and Readiness. I'm looking for grassroots solutions we can get behind. I intend to do everything in my power to ensure that Congress takes meaningful action on this important issue."

"Wow." Sarah laughed. "Usually I get arrested for speaking out about climate change. Now I've got members of Congress offering to help me."

"Only one so far. I'll see what I can do about the others. In the meantime, I'd like to meet the rest of your team."

"Team?" Sarah smirked. "We're more like refugees from the Island of Misfit Toys. I'll be happy to introduce you, though."

Irene slid the binder into her leather briefcase bag, and the two of them headed downstairs.

As Sarah and Irene reached the bottom of the stairs, the entryway was crowded with people straining to see over each other's heads and shoulders to get a good look at what was going on in the dining room. Jonny, Taliesin, and Hart were singing a simple song together, while Patricia danced with David, her automaton garden gnome, who was standing on the dining room table and swaying back and forth awkwardly to the music. Jonny was playing his guitar, filling the room with the sounds of a lute as the three men and a growing number of audience members sang along to the lively drinking tune.

> *"Oh, I've drank me some whiskey and wine and ale*
> *But never a drop from beneath the shale*
> *The glaciers would melt and the sea would boil*
> *If I drank me a drop of your dirty oil."*

The three men sang half a dozen verses, coming back to the same refrain over and over again. The serving staff struggled to make their way through the crowd as everyone near the dining room took up glasses of wine, shots of whiskey, and bottles of craft beers, some of them singing along to the refrain or clapping along to the beat. A group of about a dozen men, including Percival Sword and Edward Richard Jamison, glared in their general direction and stormed upstairs or walked out the front door. When Sarah stepped forward and joined the chorus, the gathered guests grew even more enthusiastic in their support, clapping and cheering while several people pulled out their cell phones and started recording. When they were done singing, the crowd applauded heartily.

The Preceptor appeared out of the crowd, clapping along with the guests for a few moments before sweeping his hands dramatically to present Jonny to his audience.

"Let's hear it again for Jonny Glas!" As the audience applauded, the Preceptor stepped forward and gave Jonny's shoulder a few hard pats. "Hope you and your friends have a good trip home, Jonny. In the meantime, everyone else can join me in the pavilion out back for the evening's main performance!"

As the Preceptor led the crowd out the back door, Jonny cast Sarah a quizzical look.

"Home? Are we leaving, love?"

Sarah smirked. "That's his way of saying that we should go before he makes us go."

"Aww!" Patricia pouted, picking up David and cradling him in one of her arms like a small child. "Is this because those oil men didn't like our song? Boo hoo." With her free hand, she drank a shot of whiskey, slamming the empty shot glass on the table with an impish grin. "If they don't like our songs, make them go!"

Sarah walked over to Patricia, placing a comforting hand on her shoulder. "It's alright. We should get going anyway. Don't worry though, I'm sure we'll have a fun ride home."

"Yes!" She tucked David into her messenger back and took Taliesin by the hand. "You can introduce us to your new friend, and I can show you all the files I downloaded from the super secret server in the basement!"

"It's a deal. Alright, let's go."

Sarah and her companions headed out the front door,

walking down the cobblestone path and passing between the four marble angels again on their way to the helipad. The attendant who had brought them there was standing next to their helicopter and opened the door as they approached. In a matter of moments, the helicopter sprang to life and took to the air, carrying them quickly and quietly toward their destination.

CHAPTER 14

*"Poet, scientist,
warrior, bard, diplomat
all will march for change."*
— Bertram Muhnugin, The Death of Birth

  It was a sunny afternoon in early September in Zuccotti Park. The neat rows of honey locust trees formed a vibrant green canopy over the broad granite sidewalks of the relatively small park. Several beds of flowers offered additional bursts of color in round raised gardens in the middle of the park along with a rectangular garden along Liberty Street. Dozens of people were scattered throughout the park, casually walking down the stairs and across the plaza or sitting on the benches and other flat surfaces throughout the park.
  Sarah, Taliesin, Patricia, and Irene sat together near a tall red abstract metal sculpture at one corner of the park. Sarah and Irene were on a park bench, talking and reading an article on Irene's laptop computer. Taliesin was sitting beneath a tree with a pencil and notepad, lost in thought as he worked on a new poem. Patricia had laid her tablet computer on top of her messenger bag on her lap and was typing frantically as she flitted back and forth between a dozen different online tasks. Patricia's automaton gnome, David, was slowly dragging a paper

bag full of breadcrumbs across the park, occasionally pausing to toss a couple of them on the ground near the small flock of pigeons lingering on the ground among the trees.

Sarah looked at her phone to check the time.

"They should be here any minute. Patricia, any more news on those leads you found on that computer at Providence Catalysis?"

"Oh. Just a sec." Patricia tapped on the smooth flat screen for a few moments. Her eyes lit up as the information flashed across her screen. "Ooh! Bertram Muhnugin. He's the top secret clairvoyant who retired from the Order. I finally found him. Bet he didn't see that coming! I also found another picture of the Summoner. He's the guy who causes storms. But it's from two weeks ago, so who knows where he is now. Still no word on any of the environmentalist Anomalies who turned up missing. Maybe after the Preceptor talked to us, he blackbagged the other ones on his list. Naughty, naughty! But this storm guy is still out there. And then there's—"

Sarah held up a hand to interrupt Patricia as she saw a familiar vehicle on the small side street next to the park. The Mobile Nexus slid to a smooth and silent halt along the curb. Hart and Jonny hopped out and walked briskly toward Sarah. Sarah jumped to her feet and met them beneath the tall metal statue on the corner.

"Let's do this!" Sarah grinned, rubbing her hands together eagerly. "Are you gentlemen ready for a free concert in the park?"

"I was born ready, love."

"Patricia, spread the word. Irene, you and I will be talking at the break. Taliesin, do you have a new piece to share today?"

Taliesin looked at his notebook quizzically. "Maybe. I'll give you a thumbs up or a thumbs down when the time comes."

"Alright, let's do this." Sarah cleared her throat and spoke into a microphone, her voice amplified by several speakers hidden in the trees throughout the park. "Alright, folks! Yes, this is really Jonny Glas, and yes, he's about to do a free concert in the park!"

A few of the people in the park were already looking in their direction. As Sarah spoke, more turned their attention her way. Passersby on the street started stopping and watching. Jonny pulled out his guitar and turned it on, strumming it lightly as a small crowd started to gather at the base of the stairs leading into the park. He also turned on a small microphone attached to his collar. A big green van pulled up behind the Mobile Nexus, and several people in green T-shirts walked into the park carrying signs and banners and stacks of flyers and handouts with various messages about climate change. Once a few of the banners were raised and a few dozen people had gathered to listen, Jonny took a step forward to speak.

"Good afternoon, friends! So glad you could join us on this lovely afternoon. My friend Patricia over there is spreading the word about this little impromptu gathering, so I expect we'll have a few more guests arriving shortly. In the meanwhile, let's warm up with one of my earlier tunes. This one's called Wander With You."

As Jonny played and sang an extended version of his best-selling tune, the crowd rapidly swelled from several dozen to over a hundred. Patricia blasted news of the free concert out through hundreds of online news sources, from social networking sites to blogs to online forums to Jonny's website which had made a previous announcement that there was big news coming today. People in the crowd started taking photos and video, including a few live video streams. As Sarah joined Jonny for the last refrain, hundreds of people throughout the city were hitting the streets by foot, bike, moped, motorcycle, car, and train, making their way to the small park in Lower Manhattan. When the first song was over, the crowd applauded, and Jonny took a slight bow.

"Thank you, friends. Good to see so many smiling faces on such short notice! Maybe the people of New York really do like my music." The crowd cheered and applauded, whooping and hollering in appreciation. "This next one's an entirely new piece, never before heard by anyone but yours truly. It was inspired by the very important work of my lovely lady friend here, Miss Sarah Athraigh. You may know her as the woman who told off Percival Sword on live television and lived to tell the tale. This one's called 'Here Comes the Tide'."

Jonny started playing the song on his guitar, listening to the music for a few bars with eyes closed before weaving in the vocals. The first few verses were about increasingly severe storms hitting the United States. After each verse, the song returned to the same refrain, with only minor changes in the second to last line:

> "Here comes the tide
> Here comes the tide
> To these sandy, sandy shores
> Where so many people died
> Each storm is worse
> Each car's a hearse
> Because the politicians lied
> Here comes the tide."

The final verse spoke of a growing number of people who were fed up with the storms and other natural disasters associated with climate change. It called the listener to action, praising renewable energy and ending with a modified version of the refrain:

> "Here comes the tide
> Here comes the tide
> We will sweep away the oil
> And the many men who lied
> The oceans rise
> Now so will I
> Because so many people died
> Here comes the tide
> Here comes the tide
> Here comes the tide."

The growing crowd cheered and applauded wildly. Jonny bowed with a slight smile, beaming with confidence and pleasure at the enthusiasm of his audience. Once the applause started to die down, he spoke again.

"Thank you, friends. Thank you." Jonny looked over to Sarah and Irene, who were now standing next to each other just a few feet away. He returned his attention to the crowd with a broad smile. "Friends, we'll have a couple of more tunes coming your way in just one moment. After that, we may go for a bit of a walk, if the mood is right. But first, it brings me great pleasure to introduce to you two amazing women who are veritable rock stars in their chosen genre of public policy: Sarah Athraigh and Congresswoman Irene O'Neill!"

Jonny took a few steps back, and Sarah and Irene stepped forward. The crowd applauded and cheered — not as enthusiastically as they had for Jonny, but more than a merely polite applause. As the applause died down, Sarah spoke into her microphone,

"Thank you, Jonny! And thank you everyone else for joining us today." She looked out across the crowd, smiling broadly at the sight of several hundred people gathering and listening. "I'm assuming that most of you have already heard about climate change, but Jonny here is working with us and a whole team of musicians, artist, writers, and other creative folks to help us change the climate crisis from an abstract political issue to a personal story that we can all feel a part of. People sometimes feel lost or afraid when dealing with systemic problems that seem larger than life. Either the problem seems unreal and far removed from their daily lives, or it seems like there's nothing they can do about it. We're here today to tell you that the problem is real, that it does affect your daily life, and that you have the power to create change for the better. The power's in your hands, folks. Are you ready for change?"

The crowd cheered enthusiastically. Sarah clapped and cheered along with them for a while, then handed the microphone over to Irene.

"Hello everyone! My name is Irene O'Neill, and while I may not be serving as a representative of the fine state of New York, I consider myself a servant of the American people as a whole, and the people of the entire world. With the help of Sarah and her friends, I'll be crafting legislation designed to reduce our dependence on fossil fuels and create millions of new green jobs. While I'm working at the legislative level, it's up to you to work at the community level and the street level. It's up to you to get your schools, banks, and state governments to divest from the fossil fuel industry. It's up to you to put pressure on your representatives to create green jobs programs so that we can turn the climate crisis into an economic solution. You have the power, and it's time to use that power to create green jobs and end our dependence on fossil fuels once and for all!"

The crowd applauded and cheered, whooping and hollering in support. Irene handed the microphone back to Sarah, and Jonny stepped forward, strumming a few chords on his guitar.

"Thank you." Jonny looked out over the crowd and noticed a police car pulling up to the curb, followed by a large armored personnel carrier. "That was a rousing speech, wasn't it now? Let's go for our walk a bit early then, friends. Follow me! We've so many songs to sing and stories to tell!"

Jonny led the crowd to several spots in front of several financial institutions in the blocks surrounding the park. The majority of the crowd followed behind him, growing in size and clogging the streets as Jonny sang songs and Sarah told tales about how the various financial institutions were contributing to the climate crisis and using their wealth to control media corporations and entire governments. As the crowd grew, so did the police presence, with dozens of vehicles on the ground, hundreds of officers on foot or mounted on horseback, riot police, and several remote-controlled drones hovering in the air. Finally, they arrived back at Zuccotti Park, and Jonny walked to the base of the tall metal sculpture where the concert had started.

"And that, friends, is the end of our concert. It is also, however, the beginning of your adventure. Because no matter how much money the oil men and media moguls may have on their side, my money's on you. You'll outnumber them, you'll outwit them, and you'll overwhelm every wall they put in your path. Why? Because you're brilliant, and you'll create a better world than they could ever hope to. So get to it, then, and I'll see you on the other side. Thank you."

The crowd burst into ecstatic applause. By this point, they numbered in the thousands, and their cheers echoed up and down the neighboring streets. After waving for a while and bowing several times, Jonny slung his guitar over his shoulder and walked away. As Jonny left, a local group of activists started talking about how people could take action locally to respond to the climate crisis.

Sarah, Taliesin, Patricia, Hart, and Irene stayed in the park for a while, talking to a mix of reporters, activists, and others who had been around for the performance. Eventually, though, they split up and disappeared into the crowd, meeting up with Jonny at a quieter spot a few blocks away. As he saw them approaching, he walked toward them with a cocky grin.

"Not bad for my first free concert in the park then, eh? A man could get used to this."

Sarah grinned. "You'd better get used to it. Next stop, Seattle!"

Patricia ran up to them with a big smile, while Irene trailed behind her with a concerned look on her face.

"Do I really have to give it back? Irene says I have to give it back. I couldn't get into it the normal way because it's one of the new ones, but then I used my powers, and poof! Silly humans, your encryption is no match for Anomalous technomancy!"

Sarah looked at her quizzically, then noticed a large remote-controlled drone hovering about thirty feet overhead. Patricia stared at it intently, willing it to land in the street nearby. Irene looked at it woefully, shaking her head with a sigh.

"If we get caught with that, we're all going to jail."

Sarah smirked. "They don't send people like us to jail." She looked back and forth between Patricia, Irene, and the drone. "How about a compromise. You don't get to keep it, but you don't have to give it back either. Just turn it off in an alley somewhere and see if they can find it."

"Yay!" Patricia grinned, clapping her hands excitedly. Then, she focused on the drone again, willing it to rise into the air and start flying away.

"Alright. Let's get back to the hotel and get ready for tomorrow."

They started walking toward the spot where Hart had parked Mobile Nexus. Suddenly, Sarah and Taliesin both froze, stopping in mid-step with grave expressions. The others slowed to a halt, looking at them with a mix of curiosity and concern.

"Sarah?" Hart placed a comforting hand on her shoulder. "Is everything alright?"

Jonny cocked his head to the side, cupping a hand around his ear as if straining to hear a distant sound.

"I hear something too, love. Something's gone wrong. I hear it there in the distance."

After listening for a few more moments, Jonny pointed to one of the nearby skyscrapers. Sarah immediately recognized it as One World Trade Center, the tower that had been built on the site of the former Twin Towers of the World Trade Center. It was a mostly sunny day, with the sun starting to set in the west, but a dark cloud was slowly forming over One World Trade Center. The sight of the swirling dark grey cloud in the middle of an otherwise clear sky sent a chill down Sarah's spine. For a long time, they stared at it together in silence. Finally, Sarah was the first to speak.

"We have to get up there."

CHAPTER 15

*"So it is written.
Behold now the Death of Birth!
Change unchanged by change."*
— Bertram Muhnugin, The Death of Birth

The observation deck at the top of One World Trade Center was shrouded in heavy sheets of freezing rain pouring down from the churning mass of black clouds overhead. At first, the deck appeared to be abandoned, filled only with the steady patter of countless raindrops pelting cold metal. As soon as Sarah and her companions stepped out onto the deck, however, a lone voice pierced through the veil of wind and rain to greet them.

*"Nobody knows... the trouble I've seen.
Nobody knows my sorrow.
Nobody knows... the trouble I've seen.
Glory... hal-le-lu-jah."*

The very metal of the tower itself hummed palpably in the presence of the voice, like a glass of water humming at the touch of a tuning fork. Sarah looked to the edge of the deck in search of the source of the voice — and there, leaning on the railing at the edge of the deck, she saw him.

He was a tall, lean figure with a black suit, crimson shirt, black tie, and black fedora. His body was impossibly gaunt, accentuating his gangly limbs and long, hollow face. His skin was ashen, a deep grey that hinted at a once-bronze complexion lost in a lifeless pallor. His left eye was missing, with the empty socket covered in a thin layer of scar tissue. His right eye was a sharp burst of silver shining through the dark of the storm. Two abnormally large ravens lay dead at his feet, their necks snapped and their bodies soaked in hot blood that steamed in the rain. Every once in a while, one of the birds' broken bodies would twitch slightly, as if stirring uneasily in sleep.

As Sarah stepped forward, the man's lone silver eye rose to meet her. His deep singing voice fell into silence, leaving only a sullen glare that chilled Sarah to the bone. Resisting the urge to shudder, she instead looked him in the eye and spoke.

"Bertram Muhnugin."

The man stared at her in breathless silence for the span of several heartbeats, looking right through her as the freezing rain enveloped her.

"I've been called worse."

"You're the clairvoyant who used to work for the Order?"

For a moment, Bertram smiled — a broad, cold, malevolent expression bordering on a grimace. His face lost what little trace of humor it had when he spoke.

"Order is in the business of rewriting reality, child. Who employs whom? They used me for a time, as they are wont to do. I used them for a time, as I am wont to do. Yet even now, their equations do not balance, though mine will presently."

Taliesin took a tentative step forward, moving closer to Sarah but not quite reaching her. He cleared his throat anxiously, pointing to the dead ravens and raising his voice to be heard over the sounds of the storm.

"Are you a follower of Odin?"

Bertram's face twisted into a hateful scowl. "What do you know of the Allfather, Celt? You who barely even known the names of your own gods. Why do the lost children of the Tuatha Dé Danann come to me searching for answers? Why would I dispense such answers freely when I have paid for them with the mortification of my flesh and soul?"

Sarah felt a sudden surge of warmth burning in her heart and spreading through every cell of her body. Her fear of the twisted figure standing before her evaporated, and she spoke with calm confidence and clarity.

"We come as travelers seeking your guidance. We are all lost when human ingenuity outpaces human wisdom and tears the world asunder. Your insight may change this fate for the better. Why have you bought these truths with pain of your flesh if not to share them with those who would make good use of them?"

Bertram took a long pause, eying her carefully, as if peering into the depths of her soul. They stared at each other without speaking, the freezing rain pattering all around them and leaving Sarah's flesh feeling like cold rubber. Eventually, Bertram spoke.

"You have already seen most of what needs to be seen, child. You have seen the voracious appetite of man devouring whole continents of life. You have seen the black blood of the earth sucked from beneath the soil. You have seen the alchemists create great wonders and perform great feats by unleashing the potent energy of this necromantic brew. You have seen them spew their foul soot into the air until the perturbations of wind and water and flame threaten to tear asunder the very flesh and bone of life itself."

There was another long pause between them. Sarah expected Bertram to continue, but when he didn't, she spoke.

"Yes. Yes, I have seen this. But what happens next? What can I do to change our course for the better?"

"Change?" Bertram laughed — a cold, cruel laugh that cut through the distance between them. "You have glimpsed beyond the veil, yet your mind rejects what it has seen. The deed is done, child. The deed is done. The folly of your forefathers has sealed your fate. This is the source of your urgency, the bitter bonefire that burns beneath your smug smirk and simmers in your somber silence. For nearly two hundred years, I have studied every thread of the tapestry. Peasant and king alike stand naked before me, their every secret lain bare beneath my gaze. There are many weavers, and more still who are woven. A master weaver may alter the dance of the warp and the weft with a slow and steady hand. Yet I have seen none in all the world who can change what is now woven. The pattern is all but complete, and no hand can unweave it without destroying the tapestry."

Bertram slumped against the railing, staring down mournfully at the two dead ravens lying at his feet. It was only then that Sarah noticed the blood smeared on his palms. He cupped his hands to gather some rain, rubbing them together in a vain effort to wash away the blood.

"I grow weary of this world, child. I was brought into this life by an act of horror wrought upon my mother's flesh. My body aches with the cutting thoughts of countless merciless men and the burning memory of every torture they wreak upon the world. I have sought at times to better the lot of peasant and king alike, yet peasant and king alike have left me to this, my long-awaited fate. Ask me one more question, child, before I take my final leave."

Sarah suddenly felt a deep sorrow washing over her. She looked out beyond the edge of the deck, watching the freezing rain soak the city and feeling the strands of connection and channels of causality stretching out in all directions. There was a ring of truth to Bertram's words. As she felt the rain connecting her to the imbalances that would soon lay humanity low, she found herself on the verge of tears. Suddenly, though, she felt her inner warmth resurging. A question arose in her mind with crystal clarity.

"What will happen if all of humanity awakens to the presence of this crisis and chooses to change our fate?"

For a moment, his face twisted into a cold, cruel smile. As he stared at Sarah, however, something shifted in his expression. His head cocked to the side slightly, and his gaunt features softened into a warm look of surprise.

"I—" Bertram took a deep breath, letting it out slowly with a warm, broad smile. "I don't know! So many strands of fate, all of them intertwined, all of them leading in the same general direction. Before, I could see nothing beyond the current knot in the fabric, nothing but a variety of endings devoid of new beginnings. But I see what you see, and if it comes to be, the future remains uncertain."

Sarah smiled, glancing back to her companions and looking back to Bertram.

"So what do I do? How do I awaken humanity to the presence of this crisis?"

"No." For a moment, Bertram's expression grew serious again. "What you say is beyond your reach, beyond any mortal power. But you, and those around you, and those like you, may serve as catalysts of mass awakening. You may organize an awakening network, a new power to subsume the old Order, a living engine to create a new reality."

"An engine? What—"

"No, no more questions. I may have said too much already." He picked up a raven in each hand, their broken bodies finally falling limp in dreamless slumber. "I knew that this was the end of my story, but even I could not see the change that was coming. Only you, child of Bríd. Only you. And now, with the future uncertain, I am finally free."

A look of limitless joy flashed across Bertram's face. After taking a deep breath, he leaped impossibly high, narrowly clearing the edge of the tall metal fence around the deck and plummeting into the unseen depths below. Sarah lunged forward in a vain effort to catch him, but it was too late. Even though she couldn't see or hear his descent, she somehow felt his final moment.

For a long time, Sarah stared over the edge in silence. Eventually, the rain started letting up, and her companions approached her. All of them looked as if they were searching for words, but it was Taliesin who spoke first.

"What do we do now?"

Sarah looked off into the distance, casting a wistful glance over the rain-soaked city.
"We build an engine."

CHAPTER 16

*"Change walks among us
her fingers tracing the strands
connecting the dots."*
— Taliesin Malek, The Coming of Change

The sky over Seattle was filled with an unbroken expanse of thick grey storm clouds. A light mist cooled the air, filling the city with the steady patter of raindrops falling against concrete, blacktop, steel, and glass. Traffic was light in the industrial district, especially as Sarah and her companions approached their destination. Patricia brought the Mobile Nexus to a lurching halt outside of a squat concrete building with several metal doors and several rusty loading docks. As everyone stepped out of the vehicle, Sarah looked at the building and shook her head with a smile.

"Abandoned warehouse? Really?"

Patricia laughed. "No, silly! I mean yes, they use the warehouse too, but that's not where they keep the goodies!"

Patricia led them to a large pile of gravel and an abandoned red shipping container lying by the far end of the warehouse. She skipped merrily through the open door of the shipping container and motioned for the others to follow her inside. Sarah, Taliesin, Hart, Jonny, and Irene all stepped inside, with Sarah and Hart pulling out flashlights to illuminate the otherwise dark interior of the large metal box. Patricia pulled the door closed behind them and started looking down at the floor expectantly.

"Okay, guys! We're here! Come get us!"

Irene and Taliesin looked around the graffiti-filled walls of the container interior anxiously. Jonny examined his surroundings curiously, pulling out his guitar and studying a large red "A" inscribed in a red circle. Hart placed a protective arm over Sarah's shoulder. Sarah looked at Patricia thoughtfully, wondering if she'd been spending too much time in front of the computer again, or if they'd gotten the time or place of the meeting wrong.

Suddenly, there was a loud screeching as the floor of the shipping container detached from the walls. The entire floor slid downward, carrying Sarah and her companions underground as if they were on an elevator platform. After descending several stories beneath ground level, they emerged into a cavernous chamber with a concrete floor, concrete walls, and thick steel columns supporting a grid of steel girders that criss-crossed the sheet metal ceiling. The chamber was illuminated by countless strings of white LED lights wrapped around the metal support beams as well as several dozen rainbow-colored flashing LED lights dangling from the ceiling. The room was entirely empty aside from a large steel door and a red-headed woman in black body armor standing behind an ornate wooden podium.

"Welcome to Anomalous Seattle."
"Molly!"

Patricia ran up to the woman behind the podium, softening the woman's otherwise stern demeanor by giving her a big hug. The woman smiled slightly, patting Patricia on the back and eying the others warily.

"Good to see you again, Patricia. So these are your friends?"

"Yes!" Patricia ran back over to Sarah and her companions. "Sarah's an environmental activist, and she has all sorts of powers, but doesn't really know how to use them yet. Taliesin is a healer and a poet and a prophet, but he mostly stands around being quiet! Silly Taliesin. Hart is a superhero with regeneration powers. Jonny charms people with music, and Irene is nice, but she's kinda normal, unless you count the fact that she sometimes gets people in Congress to not be evil! That's got to be a super power, right?"

"Yes, I've heard about your friends. We had a long debate about whether or not to let them come here. Please, come with me — and for your own safety, don't leave my sight while you're here."

Molly opened the large steel door and led Sarah and her companions down a long concrete hallway with metal pipes, dangling lights, and thick black cables adorning the walls and ceiling. After taking a few turns and passing a few rooms filled with bunk beds and plastic storage crates, the hallway opened up into a conference room. The walls looked similar to the rest of the compound, and the long desk at the center of the room consisted of four stainless steel laboratory tables pushed together and surrounded by over a dozen office chairs. The most unusual feature of the room, however, was a dome ceiling that featured an uncannily vivid image of a pitch black sky filled with wispy streaks of swirling clouds of stark neon colors that blended into one another and filled the room with their shifting shades of light.

"Please, have a seat."

Sarah and her companions all sat down on one side of the table, filling up almost half of the available seating. Molly stood by the door at the far side of the room, waiting for others to arrive. Within moments, an odd collection of individuals entered the room and started taking seats at or near the table. There were only about two dozen of them, but just about every age, color, gender, shape, and size was represented in the group, with each seeming unusual in some way. One was an older Eastern European man with a crisp white lab coat, threadbare brown suit, and short, frizzy grey hair. Another was a musclebound Middle Eastern woman in a flowing white tunic and black leather pants. Another was a young pale woman in a black leather jacket and jeans who was staring intently at bolts of electricity crackling between her outstretched hands. There was also a group of teenage identical triplets who were walking around blindfolded yet seemed to be able to see their surroundings without difficulty. For a moment, one of them turned in Sarah's general direction, and she suddenly felt the attention of all three of them focusing on her, watching her for several moments with their inner sight before someone else caught their attention.

After a few minutes, Molly stepped forward to the chair at the head of the table and raised a fist in the air overhead.

"We are Anomalous!" Most of the people present raised their fist and repeated Molly's declaration, including Patricia. "Alright, let's settle down and get started. And let's be quick about it. This is a special assembly, not a general assembly. Ermete, who do we have on remote today?"

A middle-aged man in a red polo shirt and black slacks looked down at a tablet computer on the desk in front of him. "We have one from Perth, three from New York City, two from Portland, and five from Seoul."

As Ermete spoke, eleven large circles appeared in the digital sky overhead, each with the life-sized face of someone from a distant city.

"Welcome, my fellow Anomalies. My name is Molly and I've volunteered to facilitate this conversation."

One of the floating faces from Korea spoke.

"I object to the entire process. These people are Order operatives! They should not be in your center and they should not be on remote!"

"We are not!" Patricia stuck her tongue out at the scowling face floating overhead. "I've been Anomalous longer than you have, and I'm half your age!"

Molly raised a clenched fist overhead. "Focus, people. We're under a time constraint here. Sarah Athraigh, are you prepared to respond to the charge that you are an Order operative?"

The room fell silent, with all eyes suddenly on Sarah.

She paused a moment, gathering her thoughts before she spoke.

"I'm not anyone's operative. Climate change is a global crisis, and I've decided to do everything in my power to respond to it. The Preceptor of Order has contacted me about the issue, but Anomalous Revolution is more in line with my activist background."

The objector spoke again, looking down on Sarah from his spot on the ceiling. "Then why did you take their money? Our sources indicate that one of Order's front corporations wired a large sum of money to your account shortly after the incident in St. Louis."

Sarah shrugged. "Their money spends just as good as anyone else's. I told him I refuse to work for him, but he put money in my bank anyway. I spent most of it on projects that Patricia tells me have been very popular among the Anomalous."

Many of the people present started murmuring and bickering amongst themselves. Molly raised her fist and spoke.

"Alright, let's hear her proposal. Take it with a grain of salt if you must, but let's hear it."

The objector scowled, disappearing from the ceiling in a blink of light. Everyone else stayed, waiting for Sarah to speak.

"I'd like your help in building an engine."

The older man in the white lab coat perked up suddenly. "Engine? What type of engine?"

"A consciousness engine." Sarah rose to her feet, suddenly feeling a rush of inspiration. "You are some of the most creative, imaginative, independent thinkers in the world. You say and do things on a daily basis that other people believe to be impossible. And there are millions more like you spread out across seven continents. If we brought all of that vision and action together into a single effort to create a better future for one and all, we could create an engine for social change that even Order would be powerless to resist."

For a few long moments, the entire room fell silent. Dozens of faces looked at Sarah curiously or stared off into the distance, lost in thought. Eventually, the Middle Eastern woman in the white tunic spoke.

"Haven't we tried that before? We're too independent in our thinking and too diverse in our abilities for such a unified effort. We do not seek to supplant Order with our own monolithic way of thinking. We have many perspectives and seek a world in which our many perspectives and abilities are embraced."

The small crowd in the room murmured in general agreement, but Sarah raised a hand to object.

"I'm not talking about enforcing a single perspective. I'm talking about a set of tools that empowers people of multiple perspectives and multiple abilities in multiple locations to work together on every vision or goal that they share in common. This would consist of an interlocking set of websites and communication spaces where people would make proposals, share resources, and take coordinated action to create change for the better. We would use any esoteric abilities at our disposal to boost its power and protect it from harm. The result would be an engine for change that would allow the people themselves to design their own future rather than letting Order design it for them. Solving the climate crisis would only be the beginning. This engine would be a way for us to work together to solve every crisis that this world faces."

The conference room filled with the buzz of contentious conversation as the people present discussed and debated her proposal. After listening for a while, Molly raised her fist and spoke.

"Focus! There's no need for consensus on this. If there are no objections, we can just form an independent committee. If you don't like it, don't join it. Any objections to forming an Engine Committee?"

Molly looked around the conference room. There were a few scornful expressions around the table, and a few people glared warily at Sarah or shook their heads in disapproval. But no on raised their hand or voiced an objection.

"Alright, then. No objections to Engine Committee.

Now does anyone actually want to serve on the committee?"

Several people raised their fists in the air, including the man in the white lab coat, the woman in the tunic who had spoken earlier, and Molly. A few more looked around anxiously and slowly raised their fists in agreement, including two of the faces floating on the dome ceiling overhead.

"Alright. A committee of ten. Not bad." Molly nodded approvingly. "Since Patricia has previous contact with Anomalous Seattle, she can chair the committee. Does anyone else have emergency business, or should we call this special assembly to a close?"

A small young man at the back of the room raised his fist. He was wearing a black quarter cap, white shirt, black vest, and black cargo pants and boots. He hopped up and down excitedly, waiting for Molly to acknowledge him. Molly sighed, rolling her eyes and glaring at the young man in disapproval.

"Nicholas, is this an actual emergency, or an airship emergency?"

Nicholas grinned sheepishly. "But it's urgent, Molly! If I can just find a few mancers to help with materials development, I can make the world's greatest airship for pennies on the dollar!"

"And nothing is stopping you from doing so, Nicholas. You just can't waste any more community time with it until you find enough support to form a committee."

"Oh, I know."

Nicholas looked down at the ground wistfully. Molly looked around the conference room once more before continuing.

"Seeing no objections, I call this special assembly to a close. We are Anomalous!"

Many of the people present raised their fists and repeated the declaration. The floating faces on the ceiling disappeared in several quick blinks of light, and everyone gathered at and around the conference table started splitting up into smaller side conversations. Sarah turned to her companions, her hands clasped together in front of her chest.

"Alright, folks! Looks like we've got some supporters."

Patricia smiled. "See! I told you they would listen! And no one has tried to kill you yet, so they must believe you about not working for Order! I still think you should have tried to give back that money. Who needs money from Order when I can get it from any ATM! Have I showed you that trick yet? It's amazing how simple those little machines are. I don't even have to use my powers unless I'm in a hurry. They just love to spit out money!"

The man in the white lab coat walked up to the group.

"Sarah, is it? I like your idea for a consciousness engine. We need to stop reacting to Order and start developing strategies and tactics to outmaneuver their thinktanks and hired guns. Thinkswarms, perhaps? Or cloud thinktanks? I've been working on a wireless alternative to the Internet that will be very difficult for Order to track or disrupt. You and Patricia would be welcome to host the digital end of the project on our network."

Sarah smiled. "Thank you! You're on the committee, right?"

"Yes, yes. I am Doctor Gustaf."

The two shook hands. Doctor Gustaf then shook Irene's hand.

"And you must be Congresswoman O'Neill! Such a pleasure to meet you. Please, keep fighting the good fight against the covert defense budget." He leaned in closer, lowering his voice to a near whisper. "If you ever want to know what they spend it on, talk to me sometime. Some good, most not good."

Irene chuckled. "I may take you up on that offer, Doctor Gustaf. Thank you."

Molly approached Sarah and her companions.

"I hate to be a rude host, but we don't normally entertain guests here. Unless you intend to join us, I'm going to have to ask you to leave. We have plenty of contacts on the surface who can help you if you're in need of lodging or Anomalous contacts."

Patricia frowned, crossing her arms.. "But Molly! There

are so many Anomalies here! I want to find out who's doing forbidden research, and I want to see all of the special abilities, especially whoever runs the elevator! Was that some kind of metalomancy, or straight up telekinesis, or what?"

Molly smiled slightly. "Maybe another time, Patricia. You take care of yourself, alright?"

"I will!"

Sarah walked up to Molly, offering to shake her hand. "Thank you for having us."

"Anything for Patricia." Molly shook Sarah's hand, leaning in close to whisper in her ear. "Order is full of liars and killers, Sarah. Never forget that. And never forget which side you're on."

Sarah nodded. "Thanks again for the hospitality."

"Our pleasure. If your plan works, we may meet again under better circumstances."

"Yes."

Sarah looked around and saw that her companions had already started several side conversations. After waiting a few moments, she raised her voice and raised her fist overhead.

"Alright, folks! Everyone who's coming with me, let's go! We've got plenty of work to do."

CHAPTER 17

*"He walked with the Fae
drunk on their wild ecstasy
tortured by their screams."
— Taliesin Malek, The Coming of Change*

    The mid-September air in Southern Illinois was heavy with the lingering heat and humidity of summer. The latest in a series of record-breaking droughts had finally broken, but the air was still thick and steamy, more so than was usual for what should have been the start of autumn.
    The Student Ecology Center was overflowing with activity. Taliesin was out in the garden leading a workshop about ecological gardening and local food systems with over a dozen participants. Irene was returning from a speaking event on campus with several dozen students and faculty members accompanying her. Hart was leaving with a dozen fellow costumed activists who were in town for a week-long retreat focusing on community activism related to climate change. Jonny was sitting out in the Japanese garden with dozens of local musicians and students, casually playing and composing music together. Sarah and Patricia were inside the center working with thirty people who were seated at various chairs and tables on the ground floor of the building. Most

were busy typing on their laptops or talking on their phones, but ten of them were gathered in a circle around Sarah and Patricia.

When Irene entered the building, Sarah motioned for Patricia to continue without her and slipped away to talk to Irene and her guests.

"Welcome back! How did it go?"

"It went well. My lectures are much better attended now that I'm a sitting Congresswoman! If I didn't have to get back to the Hill tomorrow, I'd be tempted to do a speaking tour." She looked around at everyone on the first and second floors of the large round room they were all sitting and standing in. "Looks like you've been busy! Are these the people working on the project?"

Sarah smiled. "Oh, this is just the tip of the iceberg. We've got about fifty people on-site, including an auxiliary office we're renting a few blocks from here. The alpha test of the Eutopia Engine is already live, with a few hundred users testing out the software and several community centers starting local Eutopia Circles to implement projects developed through Eutopia. In other words, it's already catching on like wildfire, and it hasn't even officially started."

"Good!" Irene smiled broadly, patting Sarah on the shoulder affectionately. "Very good. How exactly are these projects being developed and implemented?"

"The system groups people into networks according to their interests and qualifications. Projects are grouped together according to topic and scope. People also list what resources they can share: time, money, tools, skills, and so on. The system suggests connections between people, projects, and resources. The people involved do all the rest, talking online and in their local communities to propose and implement new projects using available resources. Basically, the software works in concert with more traditional organizing strategies to create a massive ecological and social justice thinktank with direct access to all of the resources it needs to turn its projects into a reality."

"Excellent! I—"

Sarah raised a hand to interrupt Irene. Somehow, something didn't feel right. She could tell that it didn't have anything to do with Irene or anyone else in the building, but something didn't feel right. There was an odd electricity in the air, like the feeling before a thunderstorm, but Sarah glanced through the windows and saw that it was still sunny outside.

"Sorry, Irene. Something's wrong. I—" She paused, tilting her head slightly as if listening to something in the distance. "Do you mind if I talk to Taliesin for a minute?"

"No, by all means." A look of concern spread across her face. "Let me know if there's anything I can do to help."

Sarah wandered outside, lost in thought. As she looked off into the distance, she nearly bumped into Taliesin, who met her halfway down the cobblestone path in front of the building.

"Sarah! I was just coming to get you. Look."

Taliesin pointed to a bank of storm clouds coming in from the south. They were still small enough and distant enough not to catch the eye of someone who wasn't looking for them, but they looked out of place in the otherwise clear blue sky.

Sarah stared at the clouds, shaking her head slowly.

"No. That's not normal, not even with the strange weather we've been having lately." She placed a hand on Taliesin's shoulder, and they shared a look of concern. "Do you feel it? Something's out of whack."

"Yes."

They both turned to the Japanese garden and noticed that Jonny had stopped playing his guitar, looking off into the distance as if searching for something. Sarah took Taliesin by the hand and raised her voice to a shout.

"Alright, folks! This is going to sound crazy, but there's a big storm coming! Gather up your things and get ready."

Everyone within earshot looked at her curiously. She pointed at the storm clouds in the distance.

"There it is, folks. That's no ordinary storm. This is not a drill. Go to your homes or hotels or whatever and seek shelter immediately."

She pulled out her phone, leading Taliesin inside while making a phone call.

"Hart? It's me. Get back here right now. There's a storm coming."

Sarah and Taliesin went inside. She raised her voice again, shouting over the chatter of various voices in the room.

"Alright, folks! Storm's coming! This dome's fairly sturdy, but if you live nearby, you may want to head home while you have the chance."

Some people looked out the window curiously while others simply started gathering up their belongings and heading out the door. Irene slid her laptop into her leather briefcase bag and slung it over her shoulder.

"A storm? Are you sure?"

"Oh, trust me." Sarah walked up to Irene, leaning in closer and lowering her voice. "Taliesin and I both have a degree of clairvoyance, or whatever you want to call it. This storm is not natural, and it's almost here."

"I see."

"Do you remember the Summoner? He was mentioned in the binder the Preceptor gave you."

"Oh, yes." She reached into her briefcase bag, pulling out the smooth white binder and paging through it anxiously. "Here it is. Five catastrophic weather events classified as Anomalous. At three of the five, the same man is seen wandering through the streets calling down the storm. Anomalous sites describe him as the Summoner, but he's believed to be an environmental activist named Rory Molan."

"Rory. I met a Rory last year at a protest in St. Louis. Wonder if it's the same guy."

As she looked out the window, the sun slipped behind the clouds. The wind blowing in through the open door was a tantalizing mix of hot and cold air, giving Sarah goosebumps as it touched the bare skin of her arms and face.

"Irene, wait here for a minute. I can feel his presence now. It's definitely him."

Sarah and Taliesin left the building, meeting Jonny and Hart in the yard outside of the Student Ecology Center. Jonny slung his guitar over his shoulder and looked at the storm warily. Hart was jogging down the sidewalk and up the cobblestone path to meet Sarah.

"Trouble?"

"Yes." Sarah pointed to the storm. "Don't ask me how, but I know that there's a man out there causing that storm. And I know where to find him."

Hart nodded. "You tend to be right about these things. How close is he?"

"Close. We can walk there. Let's go."

They walked down the cobblestone path and up the street, heading north away from the center of the storm. The storm, however, was moving in quickly. In the time that it took them to walk three blocks, the entire sky became overcast, and the air was churning with choppy winds and the first drops of change.

"There it is. And there he is."

A lone figure was walking down the street toward them. He was a young man in his late twenties with scraggly black hair and beard, wild blue eyes, a black motorcycle jacket, black jeans, black boots, and a sky blue shirt. As he walked down the street, his arms were outstretched with palms facing the sky. His eyes were fixed on the clouds overhead with a look of unbridled joy and childlike wonder. He laughed suddenly, staring deeply into Sarah's eyes with a manic grin.

"You're just in time! Isn't it glorious?"

"You don't have to do this, Rory. Let's talk about this."

Rory's eyes narrowed into a menacing glare.

"Talk? Okay, let's talk." He lowered his arms, clenching his fists and turning his gaze to the sky. "Mother nature, humble us with your power!"

Suddenly, the the wind picked up to hurricane speeds, knocking Sarah and her companions to the ground. The rain started coming down in heavy sheets, and the wind started tugging at everything that wasn't firmly bolted down, tossing trash cans and awnings and a growing flurry of debris in circles through the air. Hart placed a hand on Sarah's back and leaned in close, shouting to be heard over the storm.

"Sarah! We have to go!"

"No!" She brushed away Hart's hand. "I can stop him!"

Undaunted by the wind, Sarah rose back to her feet, taking slow but steady steps toward Rory as she shielded her face and eyes from flying debris.

"Rory! You don't have to do this!"

"I'm not doing this!" He raised his arms overhead, shouting with a look of joy in his eyes. "We're doing this! Our actions have brought an unthinkable imbalance to the energies of earth and sea and sky. If this storm didn't happen here, it would happen somewhere else. I can feel the imbalance all around me. I'm just unleashing it! Think of it as pressure valve to let off steam — and a warning of what's coming!"

Rory clenched his fists again, and lightning started striking repeatedly all around him, filling the street with blinding light and bone-rattling thunder. A nearby car exploded, showering shrapnel in a broad radius. Sarah fell down to one knee, curling up in a ball to shield herself from the debris. She could feel the imbalance that Rory described all around her — hot and cold air tumbling against each other, imbalances in temperature, pressure, and humidity with channels of causality stretching back to the distant coasts, the oceans, and the rise in greenhouse gases filling the planet with a sweltering heat. For a moment, she started to lose herself in the abstract channels of causality. Then, a flying piece of metal debris struck her in the bicep, fracturing her humerus bone and snapping her attention back to the moment.

"Rory, you have an amazing gift. We can work together."

"Together?"

Rory glared at her, his piercing blue eyes staring right through her. The storm calmed slightly as he took a few steps forward to stand closer to Sarah.

"I know who you are, child of Bríd. You and your goddess want to give humanity another chance. But there are those among the Fae who have no such desire. Humanity must reap what it has sown. As the tree falls, so the tower falls. As your cities wreaks havoc on soil and water and air, so the soil and water and air wreak havoc on your cities. As the fever rises, the ocean rises, and the land will be cleansed of your illness once and for all."

As Rory started to raise his hands overhead again, he was interrupted by the sound of a guitar. Everyone turned to see Jonny down on one knee with guitar in hand. His first chord cut through the howling wind, and the words he sang were slightly out of tune as he shouted to be heard over the din of the storm.

"Soil and water and air."

Jonny played the cord again. This time, as he repeated the first line, Sarah joined in.

"Soil and water and air."

Rory looked at them quizzically. As he stared at them expectantly, the wind slowed.

"Soil and water and air.
Some people never seem to care,
so maybe turnabout is fair.
Soil and water and air."

Jonny closed his eyes, listening to the music as he played a few more cords and searched for the next words. Rory took a step back in surprise, looking at Jonny in wonder.

"You." A more natural human look of recognition flashed across his face. The wind grew a bit calmer and the rain grew lighter. "I recognize you. Jonny Glas. You walk with the Fae. I can feel their presence within you and around you. Have you come to sing about the climate?"

"That I have, friend."

"What will you sing? Do you dare delve into the darkest depths of Faerie? Will you wander the wasteland in wistful wonder, weaving a mournful melody with the silken strands of their strangled screams? Your charm seduces the hearts of millions. If only they knew how much the Fae love this land! If only they could feel how the flesh of the Fae twists and tears under the cold iron fist of man! These storms of imbalance are just the tip of the iceberg. I—"

Suddenly, the the sound of automatic gunfire pierced the air. Hart leaped toward Sarah from a crouching position, knocking her over and shielding her with his body as a hail of bullets pounded into the street from above. Rory fell to the ground in a hail of gunfire, and Hart grunted and twitched as two stray bullets struck his back and thigh.

Sarah screamed at the unseen shooter. Hart still sought to cover her with his body, but the wound to his leg made it easier for her to squirm out from under him to get a better look at the shooter. To her surprise, there were three unmanned drones in the sky overhead. Two were circling the area in wobbly arcs at a higher altitude, but one was hovering in place with its stubby nose pointed at Rory's prone body.

Sarah rose to her feet, glaring at the unmanned droned. For a moment, it looked back at her blankly, observing her with its camera and beaming a live feed back to its home base. As Sarah clenched her fists at her side, however, a sudden burst of sparks flew out of the craft. It plummeted to the ground, exploding on the sidewalk a few yards away. She turned her attention to the two remaining drones with hate in her eyes.

"I know who sent you! I won't forget this!"

The drones quietly retreated into the distance. Sarah returned her attention to Hart, who had rolled over onto his side and was bandaging the wound on his leg. She knelt beside him, running her fingers through his hair affectionately.

"Are you alright?"

Hart smiled, grimacing slightly in response to the pain. "I'll live. One bullet nicked my femur and another fractured my rib. If I hadn't been wearing a bulletproof vest, though, that could have been ugly. Now do you believe me that you should wear a bulletproof vest too?"

"Yes. I will, I promise."

Sarah kissed Hart lightly on the forehead, rising to her

feet again to take a look at Rory's body. Taliesin and Jonny approached slowly, with Taliesin placing a hand on Hart's leg and back to accelerate the healing process. Jonny looked over Sarah's shoulder, his face souring with nausea as he saw the body.

"Not a healer in the world that can put that mess back together, love. Peace be with him."

Sarah held Jonny's hand, shaking her head with a long sigh.

"This is Order's handiwork. He was on the Preceptor's personal hit list. They must have known he would come looking for us. There's no other way they could have gotten here that quickly."

Jonny put his arm around her shoulder. "Maybe they thought we couldn't change him. His heart was lost in the storm. It's a hard place to come back from."

"Maybe they were afraid we would change him."

Sarah stared off into the distance, lost in thought. The wind slowly died down, and the steady patter of the rain faded away, replaced by the sudden stillness of the aftermath of the storm.

As the silence settled in, it slowly dawned on Sarah that the city around her lay in ruins.

The city of Gorton was a small college town in Southern Illinois. Gorton was home to over 20,000 people, most of them students at the local university. The unusual storm that devastated much of Southern Illinois that day was especially hard on Gorton, leaving the streets of the city littered with fallen trees, mangled cars, piles of debris from destroyed buildings, and twisted sheet metal dangling from the tangled power lines sagging over the main street in town. There were few casualties, but the entire region was left without power, and most of the city was rendered impassable except by foot traffic or circuitous routes through the few clear segments of road.

The Student Ecology Center rapidly became a disaster relief center for the people of Gorton. Sarah had recently purchased a mobile solar power trailer which survived the storm with only minor damage, thus providing one of the only sources of instantly available electricity in the city. Hart and his superhero trainees had already collected a large supply of packaged foods and toiletries that they had originally planned on using for a homeless outreach event the following day. Instead, they took to the streets of Gorton to clear debris and distribute supplies. Taliesin started providing first aid for various minor to moderate injuries that people in and near the center had sustained during the storm. Sarah and Patricia connected several of the computers to the solar trailer, and Patricia helped Jonny and Irene record videos about the storm publish online.

As Jonny spoke to the camera, his expression was far more somber and serious than usual.

"Half of the proceeds of my next concert will go to disaster relief for the people of Gorton. The other half will go toward activist efforts to enact policies that will reduce our greenhouse gas emissions. Because this storm was no coincidence, friends. Climate change had a hand in this, and I barely lived to tell the tale. It's up to us to take a stand and do what we can to make a difference. This is Jonny Glas, and I'll see you on the stage and in the streets when I'm able. In the meantime, thank you."

Jonny bowed to the camera slightly, his palms pressed together in front of his chest. When Patricia was done recording, Sarah and Irene clapped, while Patricia gave Jonny a thumbs up and flashed him a big grin.

"Yay! I'll make sure everyone sees this! Maybe even some people who aren't looking for it!"

Jonny smiled. "No need for your bag of tricks today, love. This one'll make a splash without any sleight of hand."

As Patricia uploaded the video, a thought occurred to Sarah.

"Hey, Irene. I have an idea. You're going to be at the big climate conference at the end of October, right?"

Irene smiled. "I'm on the Joint Select Committee on Climate Change Mitigation and Readiness. Even my political opponents can't find a good reason to exclude me from a major climate change conference."

"Exactly. And since yet another extreme weather event has hit the United States, this conference may actually get some play in the corporate media. How about if we hold our first ever Eutopia Assembly right next to your conference? We can use the beta test of the Eutopia Engine to develop some climate action strategies for the assembly to discuss, and you can present a statement from the assembly to the world leaders gathered at your conference."

"Hmm." Irene paused, lost in thought. "It's not much time to plan for a large group of people to discuss the complexities of public policy in an organized and effective manner. However, this new project of yours is meant to help facilitate the process of getting large groups of people to develop collaborative solutions to complex problems, so this would be a great opportunity to test it."

Patricia finished uploading the video and slid her tablet computer back into its holster on her wrist.

"Great idea, but not much time to pull it off! Your Eutopia Engine concept relies heavily on digital technology to organize and facilitate communication. We've barely even started the alpha testing!"

Sarah smirked. "Are you telling me there's something involving computers that you can't do?"

Patricia laughed. "Not so far! It's just hard to keep it stable when people keep asking for so many changes and most of the other people on the team can't talk to computers with their minds! Is that really so much to ask? Doctor Gustaf's been a great help though!"

"Good."

Sarah paused, looking long and hard at the storm damage that surrounded the center. The city of Gorton was known for its trees, many of which now had broken limbs or had fallen over entirely, wreaking havoc on surrounding structures and blocking the streets in several places. One large tree near the center had fallen, but otherwise the large geodesic dome and its surrounding property looked like an undamaged oasis amidst the wreckage of the storm. A small group of volunteers was starting to move the small to mid-sized branches and other debris out of the street, but it was clear that none of the vehicles in the area would be going anywhere anytime soon.

"Hart and Taliesin and I are going to be busy for the next week or two helping with local disaster relief. But all of us can spend the next month and a half doing our part to make this Eutopia Assembly a reality. When the end of October rolls around, I want us to have some serious grassroots strategies for change. That will put pressure on world leaders to follow suit."

Irene nodded. "I agree. There's an old saying: 'if the people lead, the leaders will follow'. I'm already on board, but I know that most members of Congress will only respond if there's a massive public outcry and someone there to spoon-feed policy to them. More public assemblies like this would definitely enrich our democracy and hasten our response to the climate crisis."

"Exactly. Then let's get to work." Sarah turned to Patricia. "Can we shoot another video?"

"Sure!"

Patricia took a few steps back to capture Sarah in the foreground with Irene and Jonny standing in front of the Student Ecology Center and the city of Gorton in the background. Once she found a good spot, she gave a thumbs up to Sarah.

"Okay, whenever you're ready!"

"Okay." She smiled, taking a deep breath and pausing to collect her thoughts. "Okay, let's go."

Patricia started recording. Sarah felt a surge of inspiration rise within her as she spoke.

"Change is coming. Global warming is happening, human activity is the primary cause, and the consequences are dire. Unless we do something about it right now, the very fabric of life as we know it will be torn apart. We must all come to terms with this reality and choose to change ourselves and our societies for the better.

"I'm not just talking about public policy changes. We need to develop comprehensive solutions to the climate crisis that integrate changes in our ways of thinking, our ingrained behaviors, our cultural attitudes, and our economic and political systems. These changes will empower us to create a world in which our needs are met and dreams are realized in ways that promote rather than detract from the continued existence of life on this planet.

"Join us on October 31 for the first annual Eutopia Assembly. This assembly is an opportunity for people from across the country and around the world to work together on developing real solutions and creating a better present and future for the world and everyone in it. We look forward to seeing you there."

When Sarah was done speaking, Patricia gave a thumbs up and finished recording. Irene, Jonny, and a few other people nearby started clapping. Sarah smiled, bowing slightly for her small audience.

"Alright, that's enough talking for one day. Let's get to work!"

CHAPTER 18

*"Their many voices
like strands in a tapestry
wove a world of change."*
— Taliesin Malek, The Coming of Change

The brightly-colored green and white facade of Rumi's Dance had been largely unaffected by September's unusual storm. The popular locally-owned café on the north side of Gorton had suffered a broken picture window, a punctured awning, and some water damage to the smooth wood paneling along the lower half of the walls. By the end of October, however, the window and awning had been replaced, and some of the water marks on the wood paneling had been left intact as a reminder of the storm.

In the weeks following the storm, Rumi's Dance had slowly transitioned from being a hub for disaster relief efforts on the north side of Gorton to a hub for Eutopia Engine organizing on the north side of town. The front room of the café was filled with a mix of ordinary paying customers and community activists talking in small groups or typing away quietly at laptop or tablet computers. The back room had been taken over almost entirely by community activists, with over a dozen people pushing a few tables together to have an informal meeting over fair-trade coffee and a variety of light entrées made with mostly local and ecologically grown ingredients.

Sarah listened to the large group discussion from a neighboring table, sipping her hot chocolate and eating her chocolate ginger cookie. As the discussion became more heated, she decided to join in.

"You don't all have to agree, folks."

Soon after Sarah spoke, the entire group fell silent. After a moment's pause, a young man who Sarah had met before in passing replied.

"You're Sarah Athraigh, right?"

"Yes." Sarah smirked. "Not that who I am should matter."

The young man laughed nervously. "You're the one who invented the Eutopia Engine, right?"

"Yes and no." Sarah finished her cookie, taking a sip of her hot chocolate before continuing. "I came up with the concept during an unusual conversation with a forlorn prophet on a rooftop in New York City. The resulting social network, however, has been co-created by everyone who's participating in it."

"Ah, okay." The young man glanced at the other people he was meeting with, then looked back to Sarah. "This has been such a crazy month. Did you expect it to get this big? Millions of users in the first month of beta testing?"

Sarah smiled. "I generally avoid expectations. They're very limiting. It made sense, and my guidance told me that it would make a difference, so I did it."

"Oh." The young man paused, searching for words. "So what should we do? Should we go to the Eutopia Assembly, or should we stay here and continue our local work to make Gorton a more socially and ecologically resilient community?"

"The choice is yours." Sarah took another sip of her hot chocolate before continuing. "That's what the Eutopia Engine is all about. There are nine available slots on the local bus to the assembly. Some of you presumably participated in a decision-making process to choose where the assembly would be held and how it would be run. Some of you also participated in a decision-making process about building resilient communities. Now it's time for each of you to choose how to spend your personal time, energy, and funds. Which project seems more strategically important to you? Which one will you find more personally rewarding? What projects are recommended for people with your interests, abilities, and personality? Can you participate in both without overextending yourself? The Eutopia Engine helps you analyze your options and make new connections, but in the end, the choice is yours."

Sarah finished her hot chocolate. Before the young man could ask any more questions, she slid out of her seat and headed out the door, bowing slightly to the group as she left.

The walk to the Student Ecology Center wasn't a long one, but she walked it slowly, giving herself time to reflect before reaching her destination. The people of Gorton had repaired what they could, but the aftermath of the storm was still obvious. There were stumps and patches of bare dirt where trees had once stood; empty lots where there had once been buildings; storefronts and homes that were still boarded up because the owners hadn't been able to afford more aesthetically pleasing repairs; fresh new power lines that were home to tangled webs of wire and boxes that had been patched together by the vast fleet of utility vehicles that had descended upon the town once the streets were clear. The only detail that caught Sarah's eyes, though, was one that others would have missed: the awkward patches in the street where the drone's machine gun fire had riddled the blacktop with bullet holes.

As Sarah walked, she felt a deep connection with her surroundings, tracing the channels of causality outward to points unseen in the world at large. The storm damage connected Gorton to other cities affected by extreme storms resulting from the climate imbalance; the local recovery effort connected the city to other Eutopia Engine projects; the cars passing by on the street connected to the fossil fuel industry in one direction and the extreme storms in the other direction. When Sarah closed her eyes, she could feel these connections as a tangible presence in the air around her, an unseen force weaving these people and places and objects and events together like notes in a symphony or strands in a tapestry. As she focused her attention on them, she felt them quiver slightly, their futures becoming slightly more uncertain as she chose how to respond to them.

As she approached the Student Ecology Center, the moment passed, and she emerged from her trance state. The sun had just finished setting in the west, leaving the air slightly chilly but still above average for a night in late October. Several pop-up canopies and camping tents surrounded the center, and a crowd of dozens of people were gathered beneath the canopies talking about plans for the next day's bus trip to New York City.

Sarah slipped quietly past the outdoor meeting and made her way inside. Several volunteers and paid staff were sitting in various chairs and spots on the floor throughout the first and second floor of the building. Most of them were tapping away quietly at various electronic devices, but a few familiar faces were having a conversation in the center of the room.

Taliesin, Patricia, Hart, and Jonny were sitting around a long table. Patricia was intently focused on her computer work, her eyes and hands darting back and forth between three tablet computers and a flexible keyboard laid out on the table before her. Taliesin and Jonny were working on a new song together, with Jonny playing the guitar and singing while Taliesin chimed in occasionally and took notes. Hart was on the phone, typing on his laptop while speaking into his wireless headset. When he noticed that Sarah was in the room, he wrapped up the conversation and took off his headset to greet her.

"Sarah!" Hart walked up to Sarah and gave her a big hug. "How was your break?"

"Good." Sarah walked over to the mini-fridge next to her desk, opening the door and pulling out a bottle of locally-brewed beer. "I went for a walk and stopped by

Rumi's Dance for a while. Will everyone be ready on time?"

"Yes." Hart looked at the chairs and tables scattered haphazardly throughout the room and started straightening up as he continued. "We've already loaded up the Mobile Nexus. If we leave soon and keep the stops to a minimum, we'll actually get to New York a few hours early."

"Great." Sarah opened her beer, taking a long drink before helping Hart clean up the room. "They've already started setting up for the assembly. Jonny's doing a concert on the first day, so they're expecting everyone to get there early rather than trickling in over the weekend. Patricia, how's the website?"

At first, Patricia remained unresponsive, staring at the computer screens and typing on her keyboard in a deep trance. When Sarah snapped her fingers a few times, she snapped out of it.

"Patricia, how's the website?"

"Oh, good, good." She started typing again, her eyes darting back and forth between the three tablet computers as she continued. "One of the servers stopped working for no reason, and we're still getting new users faster than we're getting new servers, but I'm handling it. There are so many computers out there just sitting around doing nothing! They won't mind if I borrow some of their bandwidth and computing power!"

"Good." She patted Patricia on the shoulder lightly. "Have you been taking breaks like we talked about?"

"Yes! Well, some." Patricia laughed. "I set an alarm to go off every two hours so I remember to take a break, but sometimes I hit snooze and keep working! Taliesin keeps making me take breaks though. I don't even bring David or Tabby when we go for our walks!"

"Good. We're heading out now, so wrap up whatever you're working on and meet us out in the parking lot. Hart's driving, so you can keep working on the way there."

Patricia nodded, her attention already slipping back into the digital reality. Sarah turned to Taliesin, Jonny, and Hart.

"Alright, let's go."

She chugged the rest of her beer, tossed it in a nearby recycling bin, and grabbed her laptop, sliding it into a case and slipping it over her shoulder. Taliesin gathered up his notes and Jonny slung his guitar over his shoulder. Hart finished straightening up the room as much as he could while it was still occupied. Then, they walked out to the parking lot together. By the time they all got into the Mobile Nexus and turned on the engine, Patricia was hurrying down the path to the parking lot with a bag of snacks in her hand and her messenger bag slung over her shoulder. As soon as she was in her seat, they pulled out of the parking lot and headed for the highway.

CHAPTER 19

*"Order responded
with velvet glove and iron fist
but could not stop change."*
— Taliesin Malek, The Coming of Change

    The clear glass facade of Javits Convention Center's Crystal Palace shone brightly in the midday sun. Hundreds of people were streaming in and out of the blocky glass and steel structure on their way to and from the registration desks for the First Annual Eutopia Assembly. They had faces of all colors and features, bodies of all shapes and sizes, and an endless variety of clothing from across the United States and around the world. Signs, banners, and screens throughout the center displayed the words "EUTOPIA" and "Here Comes The Tide" in bold letters. Even before the official events of the assembly had started, the building and its surroundings were abuzz with conversations about climate change and other social, economic, and political topics.
    Sarah walked around the first floor talking on her phone and examining her surroundings. This was by far the largest event she had ever been involved in organizing, but at this point it was mostly organizing itself. A team of over a dozen local volunteers was running the registration tables while various other

volunteers and paid staff supplied by local organizations hurried back and forth to take care of last-minute details. When she finished her phone call, Sarah headed upstairs to the top floor.

The Galleria and River Pavilion on the top floor had been turned into a massive hub for multimedia communications with people in other parts of the country and world. A collective of IT professionals was setting up dozens of small projectors and computers to create a virtual environment where two-way streaming video feeds transformed the smooth white walls into digital gateways that allowed participants at dozens of smaller events to talk back and forth with each other as though they were all in the same room. A group of volunteers was in the process of erecting a long and slightly curved cloth screen in front of the wide glass facade on the outer edge of the River Pavilion so that the IT team could project smaller versions of all of the video feeds from the Galleria onto a single surface.

Sarah slowed to a near-stop as she examined the area. The hardware here wasn't as high-tech as what she had seen at Anomalous Seattle, but somehow she found the overall effect more awe-inspiring. She stepped up to one of the digital gateways, waving at someone on the other side and touching the smooth white wall. The other person followed suit, holding their hand up to meet Sarah's. For a moment, she half-expected her hand to pass right through to the other side and touch the warm palm of the other person. Instead, she felt the cold touch of a painted wall against her fingertips.

"Sarah!"

Sarah looked up to see Taliesin walking her way at a brisk pace. He noticed her admiring the digital gateways and smiled.

"Isn't this great? Patricia's setting this whole floor up as a virtual assembly hall. Live video feeds, collaborative document editing, and some other things I've never even heard of. Some of the other computer nerds are setting up a projector in the exhibit halls for each of the issue-based committee meetings. Climate change, of course, has an entire exhibit hall dedicated to it."

Sarah nodded. "Is climate change still the most popular issue people are problem-solving?"

"Actually, when I checked about an hour ago, economic development was slightly ahead of climate change. Electoral reform was a close third."

Sarah smirked. "You know, if it were up to me, I'd put everyone on the climate committee."

Taliesin smiled. "I'm sure you would."

"You know I would. The people have spoken, though. We just have to rely on their native intelligences and trust that whatever issue they're working on, they'll consider it through the lens of this year's theme. All of those brilliant brains working together in concert are the gears that make this engine work."

Taliesin nodded. "That's the plan."

"So what were you about to tell me?"

Taliesin's expression brightened. "Oh, that! Jonny told me to tell you that he's doing a concert at Central Park after the concert here. Between our assembly and all of the protesters at the official climate conference, there are a lot of people out there looking for change."

"Good." Sarah paused, putting a hand on Taliesin's shoulder and looking him in the eyes. "Remember, though, that we are the official conference. Most of the politicians over at that other conference have been bought and sold by fossil fuel corporations. This is an effort of, by, and for the people to reclaim the public sphere and take action to advance the common good. That makes this the official conference."

"Good point." Taliesin smiled, looking down at the clipboard he was holding. "Okay, I've got half a dozen more things to take care of in the next hour. Are you good?"

"Yes. I'm ahead of schedule, actually. I'm just going to be a normal participant for the next hour or two. This assembly really is running like a well-oiled machine. You hardly even need me anymore."

"I wouldn't go that far." Taliesin grinned. "Have fun. See you soon!"

Taliesin hurried away to take care of the next task on his checklist. After looking around for a few more minutes, Sarah headed out of the virtual hall and went to look for the first official meeting of the Eutopia Assembly.

Sarah awoke with a start. The last three days had been a blur of committee meetings, impromptu political and philosophical debates, and more committee meetings, with only a few hours of napping in between. When Sarah opened her eyes, she found herself curled up beneath a blanket on a bean bag chair in the virtual hall. The large room looked less spacious and tidy than it had when she fell asleep, much less when the Eutopia Assembly started. A hodgepodge of dry erase boards, sketch pads, and supplemental digital devices had taken over the various open spaces in the room, along with over a hundred people and the projected images of hundreds more on the walls around her. The room was filled with the steady chatter of many voices discussing and debating the countless details of creating positive change on the local, state, national, and global levels. Some were calm, friendly discussions; some were heated arguments; most were somewhere in between.

Sarah yawned, tossing aside the blanket and picking up her notes. After a quick scan of the schedule and glance at the virtual clock on the wall, she realized that it was almost time for Irene to go to the governmental climate conference over at Madison Square Garden.

"Irene! Where are you?"

Sarah didn't see Irene anywhere nearby, but as soon as she asked the question aloud, she felt a sudden pull toward the large glass wall at the far end of the virtual hall. After weaving her way around obstacles and through several heated conversations, she found Irene standing next to the glass and steel wall looking out at the streets below.

"Irene?"

Irene was lost in thought, staring off into the distance with a forlorn look. After a few moments, she recognized Sarah's voice and looked to her with a weary smile.

"Sarah. Good to see you."

Sarah walked over to Irene and gave her a hug. "Are you okay? It's almost time for you to go."

"Yes, I know." She looked over Sarah's shoulder, her face warming into a smile. "This is what democracy looks like. Never in my life have I seen such a large and diverse group of people having such a complex and passionate discussion of public policy. Did you know that most members of Congress don't even read the legislation? They are the duly elected representatives of millions of people, and they don't even read the legislation they're voting on. They just do whatever their funders and advisors tell them. And I probably won't be elected to a second term because I refuse to do the same."

Sarah patted Irene on the shoulder. "I'd vote for you if you lived in my district, Congresswoman. You have a very special role to play. Someone needs to walk in both worlds — the world of the dominant paradigm and the world of change. Your position, and your openness to actually listening to the will of the people, allows us to work through the old system and our new systems simultaneously. If we can do that effectively, there may still be hope."

"Yes. Thank you."

Irene looked back out the window. Sarah joined her, wrapping an arm over her shoulders as they looked out the window together. For a long moment, they stared out at the street below in silence, watching the comings and goings of hundreds of people around the convention center. As Sarah focused her attention on the outside world, however, she felt a sudden chill. She let go of Irene, staring through the glass warily, searching for the source of her discomfort.

"Irene, how close are they to having a document you can present to the delegates at your conference?"

"Oh, they already have one." Irene picked up her leather briefcase bag, sliding out a tablet computer similar to Patricia's. "The action plans will take months to work out, but the public statement to world leaders and the general public will be ready shortly. This is set to auto-update to reflect the most recent draft. They already have a complete first draft, they're just tweaking it while we—."

"Okay. Don't ask me why, Irene, but we need to go. Now."

"Is something wrong?"

"Yes. Someone intends to stop you from attending that conference. I can feel it. They're heading this way right now."

"What? How—"

Sarah pulled out her phone and noticed that there was suddenly no signal. She grabbed Irene by the hand and started leading her out of the large room. Her eyes scanned the crowd, searching for her other close companions. She noticed that several other people were starting to drop out of whatever conversations they were in, looking around curiously or heading toward the window to see what was coming. As they left the room, they found Taliesin heading toward them.

"Sarah! There's—"

"I know. Where is everyone?"

"Patricia and Jonny are in the exhibition halls on the first floor. I don't know where Hart is. But we need to go."

"Yes."

Sarah stopped for a moment, closing her eyes and holding out a hand to silence any interruptions from Taliesin. She slowed her breathing, calming herself down and quieting her mind in the hopes of receiving guidance about Hart. She couldn't visualize his location, but she had a strong impression that he was in the lobby of the building.

"He's in the lobby. Let's go."

Sarah, Taliesin, and Irene hurried down to the lobby of the building. As they passed through the third and second levels of the convention center, there were no obvious signs of trouble, but Sarah noticed a growing number of people with looks of confusion and concern as they sensed something coming their way. Several people were trying to use their cell phones with no luck, and one group was debating whether or not to pull a fire alarm to evacuate the building.

Sarah spotted Hart standing hand in hand with Patricia and Jonny at the far side of the lobby near the main entrance. Patricia was stuffing her mechanical garden gnome into her messenger bag while Hart scanned the crowd for familiar faces. For a moment, Sarah and Hart's eyes met, and they shared a look of concern.

Suddenly, the entire building lost power. The only artificial lighting that remained was the glow of several dozen laptops and tablet computers held by people scattered throughout the first floor. The towering glass and steel walls of the Crystal Palace let in some light, but the sky was filled with dark storm clouds, leaving the room in a somber twilight.

"Sarah!"

Before anyone's eyes could adjust to the change in lighting, numerous projectiles came crashing through the glass walls and ceiling overhead. Several stun grenades started exploded all around them, detonating at several second intervals to heighten the shock and prolong the disorientation. Chaos ensued as everyone started shouting and stumbling over each other.

Sarah closed her eyes, grabbing Irene and Taliesin's hands and walking toward Hart. Her keen spatial awareness helped her find her way through the crowd, but only after elbowing her way through several clusters of dazed people. Hart was also making his way toward her with Patricia and Jonny in tow, meeting her in the middle as the effects of the first volley of stun grenades started wearing off.

As soon as Sarah felt everyone within arm's length of her, she opened her eyes and shouted at the top of her lungs.

"Everyone stay close! Follow me!"

Dozens of armed men were pouring into the Crystal Palace through the front doors. Dozens more came in from some other part of the building. At a glance, they looked like any riot police visible at political protests: black body armor, black black batons, black helmets, and clear riot shields. But Sarah immediately noticed the same thick goggles, large headphones, and noticeably thicker and shinier armor that she had seen on the shooters at the park in Chicago.

"It's Order!"

One of the black-clad soldiers heard Sarah's exclamation and spun around to face her, raising his rifle and opening fire. Sarah held her hand out in front of her, focusing her anger and deflecting the barrage of rubber bullets with the invisible force of her will. As she heard Jonny shout out in pain, however, she lost her focus. One of the rubber bullets found its mark, grazing her shoulder and leaving a painful welt as it knocked her off balance and nearly knocked her over.

Hart growled, lunging at the soldier and knocking him to the ground with an incredibly swift and powerful shove. Taliesin helped Sarah regain her footing, and Hart kicked the soldier's gun out of reach.

The group headed toward the front doors in a tight circle with Sarah and Hart in the lead. Jonny was guarding the rear, limping slightly and holding his guitar by the neck as an awkward improvised weapon. They were met at the exit by an advancing line of soldiers with riot shields and batons.

As Sarah and Hart braced themselves for a fight, one of the soldiers was suddenly knocked backward by an invisible force, landing hard on his back as his gun tumbled through the air and clattered across the floor beside him.

Sarah turned to see a young woman with a crazed look in her eyes glaring at the advancing line of soldiers blocking their exit. With a thrust of her hands, she sent another burst of invisible force through the air, knocking another soldier off of his feet and throwing a third off-balance.

"Run!"

Sarah and her companions pushed and shoved their way through the gap between the remaining soldiers, with Hart enduring a barrage of baton strikes to shield everyone else from further harm. Eventually, they stumbled through the doors and found themselves outside.

In the first few moments after making it outside, Sarah's heart sank. The entire area was filled with hundreds of men and women in black body armor. Some were patrolling the street while others were establishing a tight perimeter around the building using a combination of people in riot gear, vehicles, and portable fences. As Sarah and her companions slowed to a stop in front of a hundred riot shields and dozens of raised rifles, however, she noticed that these were ordinary riot cops, not the special strike force that was currently raiding the building.

"Wait!" Sarah raised her hands overhead, elbowing Hart to encourage him to do the same. "This is Congresswoman O'Neill! We need a protective police detail immediately!"

The riot cops on the front lines held their ground, keeping their shields, batons, and rifles raised and ready to respond to the slightest provocation. She could see a mix of anger, fear, and cool stoicism through the clear face guards on their helmets, but none seemed to be responding to her plea. After a few moments, however, a man in a blue uniform who was standing a few yards behind the front line cursed under his breath and raised a bullhorn to speak.

"Congresswoman O'Neill, please step forward! Everyone else, step back!"

Irene held Sarah and Hart's hands. "They're with me! I'm not leaving without them!"

The police captain cursed under his breath again. After conferring with a man in a suit standing nearby, he spoke through the bullhorn again.

"Alright, alright. Just get the hell out of there, ma'am. It's not safe."

A few of the riot cops stood aside and made room for Sarah and her companions to pass. As they approached the police captain, he pointed to a few of the riot cops, motioning for them to step forward.

"You, you, you, and you. Escort the Congresswoman wherever she wants to go." He turned to Irene with a shrug. "I hope you're in the mood for a walk, ma'am. Homeland Security has all of my men. They didn't even—"

The man in the black suit and tie clamped a hand firmly on the police captain's shoulder, leaning in to whisper something in his ear. The captain crossed his arms, his face twisting into a thin-lipped smile.

"You have a nice day, ma'am."

Irene nodded and waved. "Thank you, officer."

Sarah, Taliesin, Patricia, Hart, Jonny, and Irene hurried down the street together, away from the Javits Center and toward Madison Square Garden. Once they were out of the midst of the growing number of riot police, they slowed down to a brisk walk to accommodate Jonny's slower pace. Taliesin walked over to Jonny, placing a hand on his back and walking alongside him.

"Are you alright?"

"Took a rubber bullet to the leg, love. But I'll live." Jonny winced, clutching at his leg for a moment as they continued walking. "Believe it or not, I was picked on as a child. A waifish boy sitting under a tree writing poetry, and the local bullies saw fit to throw stones at me. Fancy that, eh? Sticks and stones may break my bones, but pain will never hurt me."

Taliesin nodded, rubbing Jonny's back and holding his hand over the back of his heart.

"I know what you mean. I've been there."

Taliesin started singing. His hands grew warm with healing energy, and Jonny felt an intense but pleasant burning sensation in his injured shin. By the time they reached the end of the block, his limp had started improving.

As Taliesin healed Jonny, Sarah looked around at the faces of her companions.

"How's everyone doing? Any more injuries?"

Irene and Taliesin shook their heads. Hart was rubbing his left shoulder and cradling his left arm against his chest, but he waved away Sarah's concern.

"I'm fine. Nothing broken. I can't do what Taliesin does, but I heal abnormally quickly. I'll be fine in a few minutes."

Sarah nodded. "Patricia, how about you?"

Patricia had a stoic look on her face, but as soon as she turned to Sarah to respond, her lower lip trembled and her eyes were wet with tears.

"I just need a hug."

Patricia latched onto Sarah, and the group slid to a halt as Sarah returned the hug. She pet the back of Patricia's head comfortingly, running her hand through her hair and letting go of her with a smile.

"It's okay. We've still got a long way to go, and trouble at the end of the road. But it's going to be okay. Are you ready for an adventure?"

"Yes." Patricia wiped the tears out of her eyes, her expression brightening again. "Always!"

"Then let's go!"

After a few blocks of walking, they started to come across people who were demonstrating against the climate conference. At first, it was just a few people with signs walking in the same general direction that they were. As they kept walking, however, the numbers quickly swelled. There were people with cardboard and poster board signs, others with banners, a group with drums and colorful spiral flags, people in black clothes with gas masks and improvised riot gear, and many more who simply looked like anyone else walking down the streets of New York City aside from the fact that they were raising their fists and chanting climate-related slogans as they marched on Madison Square Garden.

"The politicians lied! Here comes the tide! So many people died! Here comes the tide!"

The four riot police who were escorting them to the conference moved in closer to form a protective box around Sarah and her five companions. Some of the demonstrators looked at the group curiously. Others looked at them warily, including a blackclad teenager who threw a water balloon full of green paint at one of the riot cops and disappeared back into the crowd. Most, however, simply ignored them and continued marching toward their destination singing songs and chanting chants along the way.

As they neared their destination, Sarah noticed a drone flying just above some nearby buildings, slowing to circle overhead and follow them as they walked. Soon, a second drone appeared, and then a third. Sarah poked Patricia and pointed up to the nearest drone.

"Can you do something about them?"

"Yes!" She started typing on the tablet computer attached to her wrists. "Hmm. This is harder than usual! Maybe the Order is tired of losing its drones. I'm going to have to cheat!"

Patricia closed her eyes, slowing to a stop and reaching her outstretched hands skyward. Hart shook his head and sighed, picking Patricia up by the armpits and carrying her along with the group as she settled into a deep trance. Soon, one of the drones broke out of formation and started playing chicken with the other drones.

"Ooh! It has a gun too! I—"

Suddenly, Patricia's drone tumbled from the sky, exploding in a burst of flames as it crashed into a nearby rooftop.

"Aww! They turned it off! How did they do that? I'll have to get another one!"

As they turned the final corner before their destination, they encountered a massive crowd that was almost too dense to walk through. Thousands of people were clogging all of the streets surrounding Madison Square Garden. The police had erected a barrier around a several block radius surrounding the building, and demonstrators were swarming around perimeter, chanting and shouting angrily at the hundreds of riot cops guarding the climate conference. As the crowd grew thicker, the four riot cops escorting them led them to the sidewalk and slowed to a stop.

"We can't take you any farther, ma'am! It's not safe! I'll see if I can get any backup!"

The riot cop pulled out a walkie talkie and started talking to someone on the other end. Before the conversation went very far, however, the crowd in front of them erupted into shouts and screams as the line between demonstrators and riot cops flashed with a shower of sparks and bursts of bright light. Most people started running away from the lights in a massive stampede, but a few dozen surged forward as two figures rose into the air. A beefy man in a brown trenchcoat was slowly levitating upwards, his arms wrapped around the chest of a wiry man dressed in all black who he was lifting into the air several feet above the heads of the assembled crowd. The man in black thrust his hands wildly at the riot police below, releasing crackling arcs of electricity that were shocking dozens of people and scattering riot police and demonstrators in every direction.

Sarah and her companions braced themselves against the onslaught of fleeing demonstrators. As she strained to see what was going on in the intersection in front of them, she noticed some demonstrators starting to surge through the opening in the perimeter created by the flying duo's attack.

"There's an opening! Let's—"

Suddenly, there was a series of loud explosions as riot police launched stun grenades and teargas canisters into the crowd. The two men floating above the crowd jerked suddenly in midair as a hail of machine gun fire from a drone ripped through their bodies, putting an end to the electrical storm as their lifeless bodies tumbled to the blacktop below. A

Sarah turned to her companions, leaning in close and shouting to be heard.

"This is not good! We—"

Suddenly, there was a deafening noise coming from behind police lines. An armored personnel carrier mounted with a sound cannon was rolling forward slowly, driving the demonstrators back with a shrill beeping and blaring that caused pain and nausea in people who approached it. When Sarah realized what was happening, her eyes lit up, and she uncovered her ears for long enough to point to Patricia, then Jonny, then the sound cannon.

For a moment, Patricia looked confused. Sarah pointed to Jonny's guitar, then the sound cannon.

Patricia's eyes widened, and Jonny flashed a sly smile, pulling out his guitar. As he strummed the strings, Patricia placed one hand on the guitar and pointed her other palm at the sound cannon, closing her eyes as her brow furrowed in concentration.

At first, nothing happened. Sarah covered Patricia's ears to shield her from the loud noise, and Hart covered Sarah's ears, grimacing in pain and anger as the sound cannon slowly rolled toward them. Suddenly, the audio coming from the sound cannon sputtered and crackled, replaced with the quieter and more soothing sound of Jonny playing his guitar.

The panicking crowd started slowing down and examining their surroundings. Taliesin reached into Jonny's pocket and pulled out a wireless microphone, holding it up to Jonny's mouth as he sang.

"Peace, Salaam, Shalom!
Peace, Salaam, Shalom!
Peace, Salaam, Shalom!
Peace, Salaam, Shalom!"

As the sound cannon broadcast Jonny's words and music, the atmosphere of the scene slowly started shifting. The hundreds of demonstrators who were still in the area stopped in place, listening curiously to Jonny's soothing voice and the catchy melody of a traditional peace song that was already familiar to many of them. Soon, a few of them started singing along. After a while, they were all singing and walking together toward Madison Square Garden. As they walked, the sound cannon shifted into reverse and backed along with them, accompanying them to their destination.

At first, the line of riot cops blocking their way stood their ground. As they listened to the music, though, their expressions softened. One by one, they stood aside, allowing the demonstrators to pass peaceably through the barricades.

Sarah and her companions walked to the front of the crowd, leading the slow but stead march through the intersection and toward the entrance to Madison Square Garden. Sarah smiled broadly, wrapping one arm around Jonny's shoulder and the other around Patricia's. Before they reached their destination, however, her expression soured.

A steady stream of soldiers of Order poured out of the main entrance. Their thick goggles and large headphones shielded them from the soothing influence of Jonny's music. The first wave of soldiers rushed ahead to form a defensive line a few feet in front of Sarah and her companions, stopping them several yards short of the entrance to the building. While those soldiers held the demonstrators at bay, several in the back opened fired on the sound cannon with live rounds. Soon, the soothing song screeched to a halt.

Sarah stopped, crossing her arms in front of her chest and glaring at the row of heavily armed and armored soldiers standing in front of her. Instead of riot shields, all of these soldiers were carrying assault rifles that were currently pointed directly at the chests and heads of Sarah and her companions. For over a minute, she simply glared at them in silence, counting their numbers and weighing her options as a growing number of drones started swarming overhead. Just as she was about to make her next move, a familiar voice rang out from behind the line of soldiers.

"Sarah Athraigh, please step forward."

The Preceptor was standing at the entrance to the building with bullhorn in hand. He was wearing black body armor similar to the soldiers that surrounded him, but there was a bold white circle emblazoned on his chest. He had also removed his goggles and headphones, both of which were dangling from clips on his belt. As Sarah stared at him blankly, he raised the bullhorn to his mouth again and spoke.

"You heard me, Sarah. Please step forward."

Sarah glared at the Preceptor. "How about you tell your soldiers to stand down?"

"No." He paused, scanning his surroundings carefully. "I will, however, give you some breathing room.

Gentlemen, fall back and guard the entrance."

As the line of soldiers marched backward, the Preceptor stepped forward, giving one of them his bullhorn and slipping between them to approach Sarah. Sarah also stepped forward, meeting the Preceptor halfway between her companions and the entrance to the building.

For a few moment, the two stood within arm's length of each other, staring at each other in silence. Eventually, Sarah was the first to speak.

"Is this the part where you tell me that I'm a valuable but replaceable asset?"

The Preceptor smiled.

"No, Sarah. Not you. You are the reason Order exists. You are a brilliant human being capable of advancing the evolution of human consciousness beyond anything that most people can dream of. The musty old men who currently rule the world are but a prelude to the reality that you and your spiritual kin will create."

Sarah looked at him with genuine confusion.

"Then why are you standing in my way?"

"The world isn't ready."

The Preceptor drew his handgun out of its holster on his belt, running his gloved fingertips over the cool steel affectionately.

"Eutopia Engine. The synergistic combination of political action, information technology, and arcane arts in the service of direct democracy. Detailed, viable, and increasingly popular plans to reform election laws and restructure national and global economies. In a matter of months, you and your little band of magical misfits have inspired millions of people to believe that they have the power and the right to change the world as they see fit. You've brought us far closer to a global revolution than you even realize."

Sarah shook her head with a smile and a chuckle.

"Isn't that a good thing? Isn't that the way to solve climate change and all the other major problems in the world today? Get a bunch of people to put their heads together and come up with the best solutions for everyone?"

"No."

The Preceptor looked over his shoulder, then looked over Sarah's shoulder, his sharp blue eyes scanning the hundreds of faces that surrounded them.

"The masses aren't ready to design their own future. Not yet. Why are all of these people here today, Sarah? My people are here because I ordered them to be here. Your people are here because a handful of celebrities told them to be here. The rest of humanity is sitting on the sidelines. They're not protesting, not voting, not contacting their representatives, not even taking the time to read a one page article about a global climate crisis that threatens to wash away thousands of years of cultural evolution and millions of years of biological evolution in the span of a few generations. These are the people you want to design and redesign whole societies?"

"Yes."

The Preceptor laughed. "Sarah, my dear, you are a remarkable specimen. If the world were filled with remarkable specimens like you, there would be no need for men like me. But the majority of people in this world are simply not capable of determining their own destiny. They must be carefully guided through a rigorous program of conscious evolution spanning several centuries. Trying to make that shift in a matter of months is an incredible act of hubris."

"Hubris?" Sarah laughed. "Seriously? You're going to accuse me of hubris? You're the one who wants to control the future of all of humanity. I just want them to be able to determine their own destiny."

"You know what that destiny is? Death."

The Preceptor raised the gun to his own temple, placing his finger on the trigger. After staring unflinchingly into Sarah's eyes for several long breaths, he pointed the gun at the center of her forehead. As she felt the cool steel pressing against her skin, she eyed his trigger finger warily.

"You've forced my hand, Sarah. You've chosen to fight the system, and the system has chosen to fight back. The

Sovereign of the Council of Order has ordered me to shut down the Eutopia Engine and launch a draconian purge of all Anomalies. He and his wealthy allies would rather take their chances with climate change than let the future of humanity fall into the hands of the masses. But as you and I both know, inaction on climate change will cause a global collapse. And so, as the powerful few and the powerless many fight for the right to determine humanity's future, the world will burn."

The Preceptor slid his gun back into its holster. Somewhere beneath his cool demeanor, Sarah detected a deep desperation. As she listened to his words, her heart filled with despair. She closed her eyes, reaching out with her consciousness to feel the strands of causality woven through this place, this time, and these people. The air all around her was buzzing with a tremendous sense of potential so strong that chills ran down her spine and her hair stood on end.

Suddenly, something dawned on Sarah.

"This Sovereign you mentioned. He's in this building, isn't he?"

The Preceptor smirked.

"I'm not allowed to disclose the location or identity of the Sovereign."

"Right. You are, however, allowed to let Congresswoman O'Neill and guests attend the climate change conference. Unless, of course, this Sovereign of yours intends to publicly capture or kill a member of Congress."

"I'm in charge of security at this event. However, while we've been having this little chat, Homeland Security has declared the Eutopia Engine to be a terrorist plot by virtue of its associations with a newly listed terrorist group called Anomalous Revolution. If Congresswoman O'Neill delivers a public statement supporting the demands of the Eutopia Assembly, she will be arrested on the spot for treason."

"Maybe. But in the meantime, she will be telling the world what really happened at the Eutopia Assembly. And she will be proposing dramatic action by world leaders in response to climate change. And while I'm in there, I'll have a word with your Sovereign about how he and his buddies are refusing to take action on climate change."

The Preceptor took a step forward, leaning in closer to whisper in Sarah's ear.

"You're playing a dangerous game, Sarah." He slid his gun out of its holster, pressing it into Sarah's palm. "Be careful."

Sarah nodded. The Preceptor turned to face his soldiers with open arms and a broad smile.

"Alright! Gentlemen, these people will be escorting this delegate to the conference. Let them through."

Two of the soldiers of Order stepped aside, making room for Sarah and her companions to pass through to the main entrance of the building.

"Thank you."

Sarah smiled, turning to motion for her companions to come forward.

"It's alright. They're going to let us in."

Taliesin, Patricia, Hart, Jonny, and Irene walked slowly forward, eying the Preceptor warily as they passed him. Patricia stuck her tongue out at him, and Hart glared at him, but they all walked past without incident. Sarah joined them, moving to the front of the group and leading the way into the building.

The International Conference on Climate and Economics was a gathering of thousands of political representatives and business leaders from around the world. The main floor of the conference was held in Madison Square Garden's massive arena and featured a large stage with a several-story tall digital screen, numerous colorful banners announcing the "Developing Sustainable Economies" theme, and seating divided into different sections for different countries, with a large section dedicated to representatives of the energy industry. The flags of transnational energy corporations flew alongside the flags of the nations of the world, and some of the signs scattered throughout the arena proclaimed the importance of clean coal, natural gas, and responsible oil exploration. Most of the people in attendance were dressed in suits, button-up shirts, and other formal or business casual attire. The decorations and displays were colorful and festive, featuring photos of pristine landscapes and larger-than-life people of various races and economic backgrounds smiling, shaking hands, working, and posing with their families. However, the sudden arrival of dozens of black-clad soldiers of Order in full riot gear had put a noticeable damper on the atmosphere of the event. The middle-aged man at the microphone smiled anxiously as he looked down slightly at the teleprompters to announce the next speaker.

"The United States has played a tremendous leadership role in the global effort to balance the alternative energy sources of the future with more traditional energy industries that form the bedrock of the world economy. This leadership has been made possible by both executive and legislative action. Therefore, in addition to the Secretary of State and Secretary of Energy, we are pleased to welcome several members of the Joint Select Committee on Climate Change Mitigation and Readiness. Speaking in her role as co-chair of this committee, I present to you, Representative Irene O'Neill."

The audience applauded politely, a relatively calm and quiet response interspersed with a smattering of booing and jeering. The majority of people only clapped briefly or didn't clap at all, preferring to continue their conversations with other delegates and guests. As Irene approached the podium, Sarah and the rest of her companions followed, stopping a few paces behind her. Jonny waved to a few boisterous fans near the front of the audience. Patricia waved and smiled, bouncing in place excitedly as she looked out at the thousands of faces. Hart smiled, but his expression grew more stern as he noticed the growing number of black-clad soldiers at the edge of the crowd. Taliesin smiled nervously, waving awkwardly at the sea of faces and looking to Sarah. Sarah looked back and forth across the audience, studying the faces of the delegates and the movements of the soldiers.

After adjusting her microphone, Irene slid the tablet computer containing the Eutopia Assembly declaration out of her leather briefcase bag, placing it on the podium and clearing her throat before speaking.

"Thank you. It is an honor to speak to you today about a topic that is near and dear to my heart, a topic that affects the security of all nations and the well-being of future generations. That topic is anthropogenic climate change."

Irene turned on the tablet computer, opening the declaration as she spoke.

"Climate change is happening, human beings are the primary cause, and the net effects pose a dramatic threat to the future stability of human civilization. As you may know, just a few blocks away from this building, an international gathering of thousands of community organizers, educators, activists, scientists, and others has been meeting for the past several days to develop grassroots solutions to this and other major public policy concerns. The complexity of their discourse, the practicality of their solutions, and the spirit of their endeavor all took my breath away. I will submit the entirety of their declaration into the official reference of this conference so that each of you can consider how to apply its recommendations. In the meantime, I would like to read this brief summary."

"We, the people of Planet Earth, have gathered together in a global Eutopia Assembly to consider the many problems facing our communities, our bioregions, and the many forms of life that inhabit this world. We—"

Suddenly, a loud siren interrupted Irene's speech. The entire crowd quickly became agitated, some covering their ears as they looked around for the source of the noise. After three long blares of the siren, a recorded voice with a British accent spoke over the loudspeakers.

"Attention! Please move to the nearest exit in a calm and orderly fashion. This is not a drill."

Chaos ensued on the main floor of the conference. As the siren and message repeated, uniformed and undercover security personnel gathered in tight circles around the various dignitaries under their protection, ushering them quickly and forcefully toward the nearest exit. Some of the guests, reporters, and delegates without security details were hastily shoved aside, leading to numerous scuffles and raucous shouting bordering on a mass panic.

"Attention! Please move to the nearest exit in a calm and orderly fashion. This is not a drill."

As Sarah and her companions started to leave the stage, a dozen black-clad soldiers of Order formed a line to stop them. They turned to walk down the stairs on the other side of the stage, but another line of soldiers formed to block their path.

Sarah noticed that no one was guarding the front of the stage by the podium. There were no stairs, but it was only a four foot drop off the edge of the stage. Sarah and Hart both noticed it at the same time and started ushering the others in that direction. As they reached the podium, though, they noticed a familiar face that stopped them in place.

Percival Sword stood alone in the large empty space a few yards away from the stage. He was beaming with joy at the sight of Sarah and her companions surrounded by a team of Order soldiers. As the soldiers took to the stage and formed a tight semicircle around the group, Percival started clapping slowly.

"Bravo! Well done, my friends! Well done!"

Sarah glared at Percival, lowering her hands to her side and clenching her fists slowly.

"It's you, isn't it? You're the Sovereign of Order."

Percival eyed her warily, his piercing blue eyes sending chills down her spine. Somehow, she felt dissected under his gaze, as if those steely blue eyes could instantly discern her innermost thoughts and feelings.

"You've been talking to Truman again, haven't you? You have no idea the joy it will give me to end that man's life."

Sarah smirked. "So that's how the enlightened members of Order resolve their disputes? Doesn't sound like a friendly work environment."

Percival laughed, clasping his hands together and regaining his cheery composure.

"The Sovereign and Preceptor are often at odds. I command the future course of humanity. He delivers. When our visions differ, hilarity ensues."

Sarah chuckled. "Right. And do your visions differ?"

"Oh, yes." Percival reached into his pocket, pulling out a small handgun. "He believes that the future of humanity lies in fostering the evolution of the masses. I know that the future lies in using the masses to foster the evolution of the brilliant few."

He spun around suddenly, raising his weapon with both hands and opening fire on the people gathered at the nearest exit. The crowd erupted into a panic as Percival fired with remarkable precision, killing ten people with well-placed shots to the head. Once he was out of bullets, he lowered his gun and turned back to face Sarah, reloading the gun with a smug smile.

"You see? No harm done."

Sarah glared at him, her hand hovering over the pocket that held the gun that the Preceptor had given her.

"Brilliant few? You're saying that the rest of the world exists to serve the evolution of madmen like you who go around randomly shooting people?"

"That act of violence was not random. A higher body count ensures a greater panic. Greater panic creates a greater opportunity to expand the security state. But yes, I'm saying that the masses of humanity exist to serve the evolution of a handful of extremely intelligent and advanced such as myself."

"How convenient."

Percival laughed, sweeping his hands high overhead.

"Yes! It is convenient, isn't it? Concentrate the vast majority of wealth and power into the hands of the greatest minds of our generation, then sit back and relax as a series of natural disasters eliminates the idiots and cowards and leeches from the gene pool. In a hundred years, a few million extraordinary transhumans will have material and cognitive technologies beyond our wildest dreams. They will travel the stars, turning whole worlds into elegant paradises of their own design."

Percival lowered his gun to his side and stepped forward, slowly approaching the stage and standing within a few feet of Sarah.

"Don't you see? Even Truman, in all of his brilliance, could never grasp the glory of my vision. He sees the scenarios in which 99% of humanity dies as utter failures of the mission of Order. But in the end, that is the only path to victory. We will burn brightly for one more century, shed the detritus of a world that we have outgrown, and emerge into the cosmos as gods."

"Gods?" Sarah crossed her arms, shaking her head slowly. "You don't seem like a god to me. You seem like a sociopath with delusions of grandeur."

Percival laughed. "Delusions of grandeur? By day, my media outlets reprogram the hearts and minds of hundreds of millions of people. By night, the forces of Order move at my command, restructuring economies and governments to serve my vision for the future of humanity. I am already a god, Sarah. Now, the time has come for you to choose whether you would like to join us in our apotheosis. In my infinite generosity, I am offering full amnesty to all Anomalies who choose to join me in my quest for the betterment of the finest specimens of our species. Are you with me?"

Sarah paused, closing her eyes and considering his words. She felt a tremendous pressure in the air as the channels of causality that coursed through this moment hummed all around her. If no one stopped him, his vision would come to pass. She could feel the fabric of life burning away over the course of the next century, and she could see something emerging from the smoldering ruins of a dying world in sleek, shiny, mercurial ships that could bend space and time to travel the stars. But there was something distinctly inhuman about the cold, calculating creatures that inhabited these ships. She could feel the echo of their presence in Percival's piercing stare, manipulative charm, and hollow laughter. When she opened her eyes, the mere sight of his malevolent face made her shudder in horror.

"No."

Suddenly, she pulled the gun out of her pocket and pointed it at Percival. As she tried to shoot him, however, something stopped her just short of pulling the trigger.

Percival laughed. He raised his free hand, motioning for her to lower her weapon. Against her will, Sarah felt herself removing her finger from the trigger and lowering the gun to her side. He flicked his wrist, and she felt the gun slip from her hand, clattering to the floor at her feet.

"As you can see, my talent for controlling minds started long before I created PEN News and rose through the ranks of Order. Ironic, isn't it? An Anomaly ordering a purge of other Anomalies? The irony is not lost on me."

Percival headed over to the stairs at the side of the stage, walking up the steps and past the soldiers to stand within arm's reach of Sarah. As she turned involuntarily to face him, she noticed that her companions were similarly under his spell. They all slowly set down anything that they were holding or carrying and put their hands behind their heads, kneeling in place as Percival approached. He stroked her cheek softly, patting her on the shoulder with a hint of genuine sorrow.

"Such a brilliant creature. All of you are sufficiently brilliant to have a place in the future of humanity. Why do you feel such affinity for your lessers?"

Percival raised his gun, point it directly at Sarah's forehead.

"Let's see. Which one does she care about most? The bard?"

Percival placed the muzzle of his gun against Jonny's temple. Sarah couldn't move, but she felt her pulse quicken in fear and anger.

"Maybe. The chivalrous knight?"

He turned to place his gun against Hart's forehead.

"The computer wizard? The noblewoman? The healer?"

Percival pointed his gun at Patricia, then Irene, then Taliesin. His icy blue eyes scanned the innermost recesses of her consciousness, calling forth intense emotions and strong memories of moments spent with each of her companions. She fought against the tug of Percival's mind, but couldn't stop it entirely. As the memories flowed, her heart raced, and she felt feverish and nauseated, her legs trembling so badly that she could barely stand.

"You're in love with them all, aren't you? You would die for any one of them. And yet, you would let me kill them all before you would submit to my will. Fascinating. Let's test that theory."

Percival pressed the muzzle of his gun against Hart's forehead.

"Stop resisting my efforts to read your mind or I'll kill this one. Three... two...."

Suddenly, a shot rang out. The bullet tore through Percival's shoulder, causing him to drop his gun and cry out in pain. As he clutched at the bleeding wound, he looked down to see a mechanical garden gnome lying on its back, knocked over by the recoil of the gun that it had picked up from the ground at Sarah's feet. As the gnome slowly struggled to get back on its feet, it taunted Percival with a voice eerily reminiscent of Patricia's.

"You just got shot by a garden gnome! You can't control my mind because I don't have one! But Patricia can control me! I guess gods aren't bulletproof, are they? Hahaha!"

Percival howled in anger and pain. He picked up the gun with his off-hand, firing several shots at the mechanical gnome. As one of the bullets hit David squarely in the chest, the gnome exploded, showering bits of metal and Plexiglas through the air. Percival spun around to take aim at Sarah, but the bullet wound had jarred his concentration enough that he was starting to lose his hold on her. She grabbed his wrist, and he fired a shot into the air as they struggled for the gun.

"Kill them!"

The several dozen black-clad soldiers of Order that were standing on the stage raised their assault rifles, taking careful aim to avoid hitting Percival. He leaped from the stage as the soldiers unleashed a hail of gunfire.

Sarah raised her hands in their direction, trying to deflect the bullets with the force of her will, but she was still dazed from Percival's assault on her mind. Some of the bullets were deflected, but others found their mark.

One bullet hit Hart squarely in the chest. His bulletproof armor stopped the bullet, but the force of the shot cracked his rib and knocked him backward. As he sought to shield Sarah from the gunfire, several more bullets slammed into his body, tearing through his flesh and knocking him to the ground with an audible thud.

Two bullets hit Taliesin in the leg and abdomen. He jerked with the force of the impact and fell backward, crying out in pain.

A bullet hit Irene in the chest, cracking one of her ribs and puncturing her lung. She crumpled to the ground, clutching her chest in pain and wheezing for breath.

Patricia was grazed in the arm by a stray bullet. She grabbed Taliesin by the armpits and started pulling him away from the line of fire.

Sarah stood her ground, glaring at the soldiers of Order as bullets grazed her leg and wrist. As she regained her focus, her ability to deflect their gunfire improved, and the bullets started bouncing back in their direction. Several of them were knocked to the ground by the force of the ricocheting bullets, and the rest fell back, looking for cover where they could find it.

Sarah spun around to see Percival struggling to his feet and scurrying toward the nearest exit. By this point, the arena was nearly empty, with only a handful of people still struggling to make their way out of the building. Sarah grabbed the gun from the remains of the mechanical gnome and hopped off the stage, wincing in pain as her wounded leg slowed her down to a hobble. As she pursued Percival, she raised her gun and started shooting. After her first two shots missed by a wide margin, she realized that shooting while running wasn't as easy as it looked in the movies. She stopped, holding the gun in both hands and pausing to take careful aim. Before she could fire another shot, however, Percival motioned wildly for the crowd at the exit to come toward him. Even though they had their backs to him, over a dozen of them responded to his mental command, turning around and rushing past him to shamble in Sarah's general direction.

"Seriously?"

She lowered her weapon, sliding it into her pocket and shoving her way through the approaching mass of people. They were clearly confused about what was going on, so their efforts to restrain Sarah were only half-hearted, and she was able to break free without further injury. In the process, however, she lost sight of Percival.

"No."

Sarah closed her eyes, taking a deep breath and letting it out slowly to find her inner calm. She could feel that Percival had left the arena but was still in the building. She opened her eyes, forcing herself to run in spite of her injuries, feeling Percival's presence and following him to the third floor.

The Theater at Madison Square Garden was a spacious venue capable of seating several thousand people. The jackets, signs, and other odds and ends scattered across the seats and aisles indicated that it had recently been home to a large number of people. As Sarah walked into the dimly lit room, however, there was only one other person in sight.

Percival Sword stood alone on the stage, his features barely visible as the massive screen behind him shone with the bright colors and bold text of a live feed from PEN News. The audio was silent, but the video displayed images from the events unfolding at the Javits Center and Madison Square Garden: demonstrators clashing with riot police, teargas and stun grenades bursting through the air, strange flashes of electricity and bursts of flame wreaking havoc on buildings and cars and fleeing people. The video was framed by a large block of text declaring "TERROR IN NYC" with the subtitle "ANOMALOUS REVOLUTION TO BLAME".

As Sarah approached the stage, Percival raised his arms with a smile, wincing in pain as his injured shoulder limited his mobility.

"Welcome!"

Sarah raised her gun, holding it with both hands and taking aim at Percival's chest. As she slid her finger over the trigger, however, something held her back.

"Sarah, Sarah, Sarah. Have you learned nothing?"

He lowered his arms, waving his palm dismissively at Sarah's gun. She lowered it slowly, glaring at him as she stood frozen in place.

"I am still in control. Your mind is mine to mold as I see fit. There is a core of raw power in you that I could sculpt into a thing of beauty if given the chance. Alas, the risk is too great."

He pointed at her hand, directing it with his mental command. Slowly, she raised the gun and pointed it at her own head, pressing the cold steel against her temple.

"Part of you wants to continue this vain struggle to change the future. But part of you has grown weary of this world. You have foreseen the deaths of billions of people and the collapse of an entire planet's living ecology. You can't bear the thought of experiencing firsthand what you have seen in fleeting glimpses. So sleep, my dear child. Sleep, and return to your Goddess. She will welcome you with open arms, and you will never know pain again."

As Percival spoke, Sarah felt a tremendous sorrow wash over her. Her heart raced, her body trembled, and she felt tears streaming down her cheeks. Her finger slid over the trigger, and she pressed her muzzle of her gun firmly against her temple.

Just as she was about to pull the trigger, something held her back.

The images that Percival was evoking in her consciousness faded from her mind. Suddenly, other images started coming to mind: the faces of her companions; long days and nights spent camping and hiking through the wilderness; the growing sense of connection she felt to the people and places that surrounded her; her dreams and visions of a future very different than the one that Percival was describing.

Sarah slowly slid her finger off of the trigger. As she lowered her weapon and slid it into her pocket, a look of confusion spread across Percival's face.

"No." He stepped back slowly, reaching toward the cold video screen behind him for comfort. "No, it's not possible. You can't do that."

Sarah started walking slowly toward Percival, her eyes burning with fierce rage.

"You will never hurt anyone again. You will learn what you have done, and you will never hurt anyone again."

Sarah reached into Percival's mind, raising her hand and clenching her fist as she flooded his consciousness with images and experiences of the consequences of his actions. She felt the channels of causality humming all around her and coursing through her as she blasted his mind with the echoes of everything he had brought into the world: the burning hate and fear created by his media empire; the lives destroyed by midnight raids and drone attacks and secret prisons; the countless indescribable experiences and evolutionary potentials lost to the ages as wantonly destructive industries caused wave after wave of mass extinction and destabilized the ecosystems of an entire world.

"No. No. No!"

Percival screamed, clutching at his head and falling to the ground in a trembling heap. He slipped into a deep trance, dreaming deeply and experiencing firsthand moment after moment of the suffering his actions had created.

As Sarah watched him writhe in agony, she felt a sickness in the pit of her stomach. She sighed, shaking her head slowly. She had stopped pushing thoughts into his mind, but there was no undoing what she had done, and no coming back from the place she had sent him.

Sarah walked over to the stairs and stepped onto the stage, looking down at Percival mournfully. She pulled the gun out of her pocket, holding it in both hands and taking careful aim. This time, there was no hesitation. She pulled the trigger, emptying all of her bullets into his writhing form and continuing to click the trigger when the gun was empty.

When Sarah was done, a sudden stillness settled over

the theater. Percival lay motionless at her feet, his body coming to rest as the thoughts left him. She dropped the gun, and her nausea swelled, causing her to vomit suddenly. After spitting out the lingering taste of bile, she walked to the edge of the stage, sat down, and cried.

CHAPTER 20

*"This is not the end.
This is just the beginning.
We must be the change."*
— Taliesin Malek, The Coming of Change

"We are gathered here today to honor the tragic passing of a great hero."

As Sarah spoke, she looked down at the small marble headstone, running her finger over the thorns of the long-stemmed rose she held in her hand.

"If it weren't for his noble sacrifice, I wouldn't be standing here today. When push came to shove, he gave his life so that others might live. And for that, he will always be remembered as a hero."

Sarah bent down and placed the rose gently on the headstone. After a moment's pause, she stood back up, placing her hand over her heart with a smile.

"Goodbye, David. You were the bravest little garden gnome in all the world."

Sarah chuckled, covering her mouth and trying to stifle her laughter. Hart laughed heartily. Jonny smiled. Taliesin and Irene both turned away slightly to hide their expressions. Patricia scowled, punching Sarah's bicep.

"Hey! You said you would be serious! He was my only friend before I met you!"

"I know, I know." Her laughter subsided, and her face settled into a soft smile. "And I do feel grateful for the little guy's sacrifice. I'm just relieved that it wasn't one of us!"

David's grave was near the Japanese garden at the Student Ecology Center. After finishing David's eulogy, they all walked the short path back to the center and went inside.

The Student Ecology Center looked much emptier than it had in the months leading up to the Eutopia Assembly. The Department of Homeland Security had raided the center while Sarah and her companions were out of town, confiscating all digital devices, paperwork, money, and almost a third of the library. There was no longer any money to pay any staff, and the handful of volunteers who hadn't been driven away by the sudden arrests and raids on their homes were off holding a fundraiser in a park on the other side of town. All that remained were two couches, three small tables, several stacks of chairs, and an empty desk.

Sarah walked over to one of the stacks of chairs and grabbed two chairs to place around the central table. Taliesin and Hart followed suit, and Sarah and her companions sat down around the table.

"So." Sarah smiled broadly, clasping her hands together in front of her heart. "I know that we all have places to go, but I thought we should check in again before we go our separate ways. Taliesin, why don't you start."

"Okay." Taliesin pulled a small notepad out of his pocket and started paging through his notes. "I'm still recovering from my wounds, but I'm up and about again, so that's good. Being a healer has its advantages. Now that I'm ready to travel, I'll be spending a few weeks with Patricia on her tour of what's left of Anomalous Revolution."

"Good. How about you, Patricia?"

"I'm fine! And I'm excited about our trip!" She started tapping on her tablet computer as she spoke. "The raids on Anomalous Revolution were awful! Hundreds of people arrested, hundreds more disappeared, probably dead if you ask me. It's like the Order pressed a big shiny doomsday button and blew it all up! But they didn't get everyone. And they didn't stop the Eutopia Engine! People are still using the online network to develop solutions to all sorts of activist causes, including the recent raids. They've gone underground for now, but they're discussing ways that we can involve as many people from the general public as possible without getting everyone arrested. I'm going to meet with some of them and help them rebuild local groups and make sure the servers are ready for the next raids. Can you believe Homeland Security declared us a bunch of terrorists? It's crazy! They're the terrorists. They're the ones—"

"Yes, yes Patricia." Sarah smiled, raising a hand to interrupt Patricia. "You don't have to tell us. We know. Hart, how about you?"

"I'm alright." He rubbed the spots on his chest where the bullets had hit him. "I'll be staying here with Sarah. I still feel a little sore and strange, but it's hard to believe I nearly died a few days ago. Thank you for all of the help in recovering, Taliesin."

Taliesin smiled. "You did most of the work. I've never seen anyone recover like you do. I'm a healer, and you heal faster than I do."

"How about you, Jonny?"

"I'm in a bit of a pickle, love. My trusty tool of the trade somehow survived our little brush with the great and powerful Oz, but the rest of my worldly wealth is gone. Seems the men in suits and ties can't help but seize the assets of every wealthy musician who happens to be accused of associating with terrorists. Guilty until proven innocent, it seems. Same goes for my record label, which fancies rock stars who look like rebels but doesn't have the stomach for the real deal." Jonny leaned back in his chair, propping his feet up on the table with a smile. "But have no fear, love. As long as I have my guitar, I'll get by. Let me know the next time you'd like me to play a gig, and I'll be there."

"Thank you. How about you, Irene?"

"Well, first of all, I've decided that I would never again like to experience a punctured lung."

Everyone laughed. Irene touched her freshly healing wound, rubbing it gently.

"Seriously though, thank you, Taliesin, for sharing your healing arts with us."

"I'm glad I could help."

"As for the rest, there's good news and bad news." Irene leaned back in her chair with a sigh. "The good news is that for the time being, you can still call me Congresswoman O'Neill. The bad news is that the House Ethics Committee is currently debating whether to censure or expel me. They may, in fact, have enough votes to do the latter. I'll be leaving on the next flight to D.C. With a little luck, I may be able to keep my job and stay out of jail."

Jonny raised his hand and spoke.

"Speaking of jail, love, why aren't we in it? I don't mean to toot our horn, but we're the closest thing to leaders that this little leaderless project of yours has. Why not just nab us all and be done with it?"

"Honestly, I don't know." Sarah looked out the window, her eyes following the cars driving by the center. "I have to assume that we're all being watched very carefully. And I have to assume that the Preceptor is still out there somewhere, and still wants us to work on the issue of climate change, otherwise we'd all be dead right now."

"Boo!" Patricia stuck out her tongue and thumbed her nose at the windows. "The Preceptor probably didn't arrest us because he's too busy blackbagging the most awesome people in the world! I don't care if he's working on climate change too. You should melt his brain and shoot him in the head like you did to the Sovereign! Bang bang bang!"

Sarah glared at Patricia.

"Don't talk like that. I'm not proud of what I did to the Sovereign. I will never do that to anyone else. Ever."

Patricia crossed her arms. "Well, if the Preceptor's such a nice guy, he needs to leave the Order, or make the

Order surrender or something. No more secret wars against the people of the world!"

"Yes." Sarah sighed, taking a moment to relax before continuing. "Anyway, Irene has to catch her flight, so we'd better get going. It'll be at least a few weeks before we all see each other again, so let's be sure to stay in touch. And be safe out there."

Sarah stood, extending her arms out for a group hug. Everyone stood up and approached her, and they all hugged each other in one big group, holding each other for a long moment before parting ways. Taliesin, Patricia, and Irene headed out to the Mobile Nexus. As Hart and Jonny headed toward the door, they noticed that Sarah wasn't following. They paused in the doorway, and Hart looked back to her expectantly.

"Rumi's Dance?"

"You two go ahead. I'll meet you there."

Hart shrugged, and the two men walked out the door and headed to the parking lot. Once they were gone, Sarah sat down on her empty desk and stared out the window, lost in thought. After a while, she closed her eyes, opening her inner senses to her surroundings.

Sarah felt the presence of a tremendous potential slumbering in the little patch of earth on a busy corner in the sleepy college town of Gorton, Illinois. Echoes of activist moments from decades past lingered in the smooth wood of the geodesic dome, the soil underfoot, the water in the pond, and the stone beneath the soil. Numerous channels of causality intersected at this point in space and time, creating tremendous opportunities for change. Many unusual and remarkable people had been drawn here and would continue to be drawn here. Each brought with them slightly different strands of influence and experience, strands which blended into chords when played together, and chords which stretched into symphonies when played in the right order. She could feel the potential for change, a self-playing symphony that danced within her, reverberated all around her, and echoed through the cosmos.

As Sarah sat in her trance, she was suddenly

distracted by someone approaching the center. At first, she sensed his presence while her eyes were still closed — a bright, sharp, tightly contained consciousness inserting itself for a moment into an otherwise more fluid dance. When she opened her eyes, she saw a man walking through the front door of the building and approaching her.

The man at the door was in his mid-twenties with shoulder-length brown hair, a lime green shirt, khaki pants, and hiking boots. At first, Sarah wasn't sure why he seemed familiar. Then, she realized that it was the same man who had come by the center on the day that she'd met Taliesin.

Sarah gave the man a wary look. The man seemed not to notice, smiling broadly and extending his hand to her with a smile.

"Hi there!"

"Hi." Sarah paused, shaking his hand slowly. "How can I help you?"

"Oh, I'm just here to return a book. Can I give it to you?"

"Yes, I'll take it."

The man handed a hardcover book to Sarah. He pressed her hands together around the book for a moment, holding them there for longer than she expected.

"Great read. I highly recommend it."

Without another word, the man turned away and walked out the door. Sarah waited for a while after the man had left, then opened the book.

Most of the pages of the book had been hollowed out to conceal a stack of hundred dollar bills, a gold credit card, and a post-it note with the words "Climate Change" on one side and "Be Careful" on the other.

Sarah smirked, closing the book without removing its contents. She slid it into her pocket and rose to her feet, heading toward the door. After taking one last look around the center, she closed the door and locked it behind her, heading down the cobblestone path and onto the sidewalk.

As she walk toward Rumi's Dance, she felt a cold wind blowing across the warmth of her face. Her thoughts wandered through the many courses of action and possible futures that lay before her. She closed her eyes and breathed in and out slowly, walking forward in calm silence and listening for the coming of change.

ABOUT THE AUTHOR

Treesong is an author, community organizer, talk radio host, and Real Life Superhero living in Southern Illinois. He grew up in the Chicagoland area and moved to Carbondale, Illinois to study philosophy at Southern Illinois University. Through his academic studies and activism, he became involved in the environmental movement, eventually changing his name to Treesong to reflect his newfound Earth-centered spirituality.

In addition to Change, Treesong has written several books of poetry, articles on environmental and spiritual topics, and Revolution of One, a beginner's guide to personal empowerment and community organizing.

For more information, visit Treesong's official website at treesong.org.

Made in the USA
Charleston, SC
05 May 2013